SWORD OF THE SPIRIT

SEQUEL TO SWORD OF THE HEART

SWORD
OF THE SPIRIT

EMILIO DIAZ

iUniverse®

SWORD OF THE SPIRIT
SEQUEL TO SWORD OF THE HEART

iUniverse books may be ordered through booksellers or by contacting:

iUniverse
1663 Liberty Drive
Bloomington, IN 47403
www.iuniverse.com
1-800-Authors (1-800-288-4677)

Because of the dynamic nature of the Internet, any web addresses or links contained in this book may have changed since publication and may no longer be valid. The views expressed in this work are solely those of the author and do not necessarily reflect the views of the publisher, and the publisher hereby disclaims any responsibility for them.

Any people depicted in stock imagery provided by Thinkstock are models, and such images are being used for illustrative purposes only.
Certain stock imagery © Thinkstock.

ISBN: 978-1-4917-7545-5 (sc)
ISBN: 978-1-4917-7546-2 (hc)
ISBN: 978-1-4917-7544-8 (e)

Library of Congress Control Number: 2015915933

Print information available on the last page.

iUniverse rev. date: 10/6/2015

SPECIAL THANKS AND DEDICATIONS

There are so many people that were a part of making this book a reality and it would be impossible to list them all, but below are a few who made this dream possible.

My Lord and Savior, Jesus Christ

My Family, especially my Mother, Coralia, for putting up with me, my Wife, Amy, who sat with me, supported and helped me iron out a lot of details, and my children, Arturo, "Artie", Xavier "Javi" and Emma, for giving me so much positive energy through their smiles and love

The Presidio's staff, for being available at odd hours and answering random questions about this historic landmark

The Seminole Tribe of Tampa, Florida (for protecting and symbolizing our state's heritage and natural history)

Wiliam J. Hall, Author of "The Haunted House Diaries", for help with many aspects of writing and being a good friend and colleage

James Fuller, Author of "What Remains", for help with grammar, word usage and being a true friend and colleague

Barb Von Pagel, for help with information regarding the Presidio and San Francisco

Holden Strianese, for providing the official theme song for the book, "In Search of the Raven"

Alexa Model and Talent Agency, for supporting my creative career

Contents

PROLOGUE

The biting cold wind did little to soothe the young woman's aching body. She stood upon the deck of the ship, Inferno, hoping that somehow the ship would turn around and take her back to her homeland, now very far away. She hoped that all the events that had transpired had been just a silly dream. Emperor Meiji did NOT ask her, Sen-hi Sakeda, to go to the Western Barbarian's homeland and be his envoy there. She did not just say goodbye to her former male consort, Samurai and friend, Toshiro. She did not get on board such a ship, infested with the most disgusting human vermin on Earth. *No*, Sen-hi thought to herself, *I did not do any of these things*. Soon enough, she would wake up from this terrible nightmare and be in the kitchen of her old restaurant, awaiting orders from her sister, Megumi.

But no matter how many times she attempted to deny it, reality was a hard master to serve. It slapped her awake from her daydreaming any time a wave would crash against the side of the weathered ship, causing her stomach to churn in protest, or when she heard the incessant babbling of some of the sailors. She could not understand everything they were saying, but she was sure that they were talking about her. Sen-hi could read body language very well, given that she was a Samurai. She wanted so much to take her sword and slice them into a million pieces, and well she could, for she was the one that single-handedly defeated over 50 men at once using the fabled Sakeda Ryu sword fighting style that her father, the legendary Masotoshi

Sakeda, passed down to her. These uncouth sailors were no match for the legendary Sakeda blade. Sen-hi secretly hoped one of them would find the courage to face her openly, but she knew that they wouldn't. They were weak, after all; Americans mostly and not experienced in close quarters sword combat.

The Captain of the ship stood apart from them all though. He was reliable and tough not unlike the Inferno, which had seen many winters and summers, cargo and passengers fit to busting at times, traveling to exotic ports in Mexico, South America and back to America for berthing. Sen-hi took in his broad shoulders and bushy mustache and smiled. He looked like he had seen many lands and, perhaps, many battles. His face was weathered and, maybe even tired. The Captain must have felt her gaze, for he changed his gait and direction and approached Sen-hi with a gentlemanly smile across his craggy face.

"Pay no heed to these men, fair lass. They are but hired help and no help if'n I have anything to say about it." Sen-hi watched his lips move but could not understand most of the words coming out of them. She politely nodded and turned her attention back to rolling waves, a thick mist had gathered nearby and shadows could be seen playing games of chance with the senses. "If'n there's anything t'all ya need, ya jest be needing to call on me, Captain Harrington, and I'll come to yer aid lickety split." The Captain suddenly became perplexed as to why this girl wasn't responding to him, but then Sen-hi's confused glance illuminated him. "Beggin' yer pardon, my dear. I forgot you..." Captain Harrington cleared his throat and then something miraculous happened. Sen-hi understood him. He was speaking almost perfect Japanese.

"I apologize for my ignorance, my dear. My pride betrayed me and I thought you spoke English."

Sen-hi's tone gave away her surprise. "It is quite all right, Captain. I am honored that you would take time to converse with me."

"Think nothing of it. As I said earlier, my name is Captain James Harrington and this is my ship, The Inferno. The crew here is hired help, but they will do their job well, or heaven help me, I'll string them to the mast, I will!" The Captain's eyes sneered at the unkempt sailors loafing around the deck. With a shout in English, they sprawled across the deck of the ship, each man to his station.

"Miss, we have been out at sea for a long period of time. I do hope your government was gracious enough to give you some sort of preparation for what may lie ahead."

Sen-hi wondered at Harrington's statement. What did he mean, 'what may lie ahead'?

"The sea is a truly harsh mistress, it is said, and she is not picky about who travels on her. There are many-a-times that we run across bloodthirsty pirates and…"

Sen-hi stopped his words with a tap of her sheathed sword on the deck.

"I assure you, Captain James Harrington, if there are any intruders on your ship, they will not live to see another wave."

The Captain seemed to be more at ease now that it was revealed that a true Samurai was on board his ship. All this time he thought her an expensive gift for some high and mighty land owner in San Francisco. But, he recalled, Samurai are predominately male. He wondered how a girl, and such a young one at that, could have gotten into that bloody trade. No sooner had the breath formed to ask her the question when one of his sailors shouted, "There be Pirates!"

"You'd best be tying yourself to the mast." The Captain said, handing Sen-hi a rope and pointing to the center of the ship.

The warning shot splashed dangerously close to The Inferno and rocked the Captain to action. Captain Harrington had played this game far too often and knew that the next shot would hit the ship. He rushed to the wheel and pushed aside his helmsman. "I'll take this, get ye to the cannons, lad!" His callused hands gripped the steering wheel and swung it with a force to match any three men's strength. The Inferno tilted in its wake, heading straight towards the massive pirate ship off its starboard side.

"Ready yerselves fer the boarding party gents!"

Captain Harrington's voice carried throughout the deck and Sen-hi braced herself against the mast as a thunderous explosion, then a crash of water, ripped through the side of the ship she had just been on. She had never experienced anything like this before and was truly scared for her life for the first time since she lost to the evil warlord, Akushin Hiruma. Her memory fluttered with visions of rice mixed with blood, the result of an old injury that he inflicted, as another blast sent splinters of wood flying towards her. Thinking it best to untie herself, she quickly unsheathed her sword and cut the rope in one swing. A huge jagged piece of wood slammed against the mast and she barely dodged out of its way. The shock of the next blast was so great that it catapulted her body across the ship. She screamed in pain as her body crashed against the hard unforgiving wooden upper deck.

"Told you to tie yourself to the mast, young one." The Captain said to her in her language.

Meanwhile, the pirates had already thrust multiple lines of rope onboard The Inferno and were beginning to make their invasion.

"Steel yourself, my dear. Pirates are known to kill man and woman alike, yes, even children!"

"Let them come. I swear I will make them pay for what they just put me through." The sight of the pirates jumping onto The Inferno's deck quickened her pulse and the stamina to stand up and face them arose in her.

The first group of pirates had what looked like small muskets. Sen-hi had seen similar ones like these in the battle in Edo, but these looked smaller. She figured she could disarm them easily. She was proven wrong.

The pirates let out a barrage of bullets around the ship and Sen-hi was grazed in her leg by one of the shots. She let loose a cry of anger and sliced the first pirate she saw in half. When the others saw this impossible feat, they fired wildly in her direction but, luckily for her, they missed by a hair. Sen-hi was simply too fast for them. With one stroke, she sheathed her sword and jumped in the middle of the closest group. Her eyes flashed with anger as she saw their guns waving in the air near her. Within a fraction of a second, she jumped backwards and performed the Mantu Ryu Sen, a maneuver that utilizes the sharp edge of her sword and the powerful arc of her leap to take out multiple attackers. It proved to be formidable, for of the ten pirates immediately surrounding her, only two made it out with their heads intact.

"Take out that one!" The pirate Captain pointed at Sen-hi and waved his rusty cutlass, charging towards Captain Harrington, who was in the midst of fending off some pirates, recently relieved of their weapons by the seasoned Captain.

Even in this situation, Sen-hi knew exactly what her next priority was. Protect the king. In this case, of course, that meant her new friend, Captain James Harrington. Her sword glistened with hunger for new blood as she wiped it clean. Her leg was injured, but she still managed to make it to the upper deck where she was thrown to earlier.

Captain Harrington dispatched one of the pirates in front of him and was shocked when he saw the other pirate collapse for no reason. His shock quickly vanished when he witnessed Sen-hi appear where the other pirate was just standing.

The pirate Captain appeared out of the smoke rising from one of the holes on deck, so conveniently made by one of the cannonballs that pierced through the ship's hull. The Captain's sword first met with Sen-hi's blade, but it was no match for her katana. Sen-hi's sharp katana sliced the pirate Captain's blade in two as easily as if it was part of the incorporeal air around her. The pirate Captain yelled in protest and surprisingly kicked Sen-hi in the crotch. The unexpected jab did hurt, but, being a woman, Sen-hi didn't react the way that the pirate had intended. Instead, she delivered a stab to the pirate's shoulder blade and stepped aside as Captain Harrington delivered the final blow.

Having dispatched of the rest of the pirates, the Captain of the Inferno made his way around the ship to assess the damage with Sen-hi walking beside him. One of the sailors said something that Sen-hi did not understand to the Captain and his face took on a most somber look.

"It seems as if we will not be making it to the port in Mexico, m'dear. The ship must be taken to the nearest port and repaired."

"Where is that, Captain?"

"We are not to be heading back, for that would put us into more danger. No, the nearest harbor is in Monterey, California. We'll have to stop there, repair the ship and await orders. I'm afraid your diplomatic mission will have to wait. Perhaps you can talk to my friend there, Jacob. He may be able to get you a transport to Mexico."

Sen-hi did not like this turn of events, but did not see any other alternative. Her frustrated gaze lingered for a moment on the floating and empty pirate ship near them and she immediately knew what to do.

"Pardon me, Captain Harrington?"

"Yes, m'dear?"

"If you permit me, I have an idea."

CHAPTER ONE

NEW FRONTIER

Harbor master Jacob Miller had seen some pretty amazing things on his watch in Monterey Harbor in the fifteen years he had been stationed there. He had seen ships large enough to fit half a village coast in to his port and still manage to fit in the docks. He had heard stories of merfolk and gigantic sea monsters attack boats at random and eat unsuspecting victims whole, leaving no trace behind but the tale itself. But this morning, he admitted to himself that he had seen the most unusual sight of all. A pirate ship was actually coming in to dock at San Francisco Harbor.

The ship had the standard skull and crossbones tied on the mast and, on top of that, the American flag, which could only mean that this ship had been taken over by a crew of professional naval officers. Naval Maritime Law had only just been passed a decade ago, what with the Barbary Coast Wars and all, still, being cautious never hurt. Jacob called out to the stevedores on the dock to clear the way and instructed all the nearby officers and naval personnel to be on standby. The harbor patrolmen noticed the intimidating ship come into dock and assembled into a perfect two-line formation. The ship was almost within firing range. The Seaman whose rank was closest to Captain shouted rank and file orders up and down the firing line. The Seamen, one line on bended knee, the other standing at attention behind them, had their rifles at the ready. The ship threw the mooring line off the side and Jacob watched with awe as another unbelievable sight met his eyes. His old friend Captain James Harrington peered over the side, looking straight at him.

"Ahoy there, ya scallywag, Jacob! I understand ye be looking fer a new addition to yer antique collections! Would this be suitin' ye?"

The two men exchanged hearty laughter over two mugs of ice cold beer inside the local inn, The Spray. The inn had been hastily built to accommodate the massive swarm of prospectors, immigrants and wayfarers that had come into the city of Monterey ever since the rush had started for Gold mining back in the 40's. The floors and walls jumped and quaked with excitement from all the giddy 49'ers scoring it big on the mountain side, dancing from all the nuggets raining down in a cascade of sweet providence. They creaked and groaned with the weight of the thousands upon thousands of weary souls needing a rest after losing everything to the pox or having just barely survived an Indian attack on their wagon trains near Little River. The two men blended in well with the simple furnishings and lively crowds.

"So the varmint kicked our little Samurai here straight in the unmentionables and, bein' a woman an' all, she didn't flinch. No sir, just up and sliced his sword in twain!" Captain Harrington swished his mug in the air, attempting to mimic Sen-hi's sword movements and gulped down a swig. He had been at sea far too long, he knew, and he needed this rest.

"But, James, where is the Inferno?" Jacob asked.

Harrington followed his line of site to the officers on the harbor dock processing the inventory from the captured pirate ship.

"Ar, she mayhap be on the bottom of the briny blue, me bucko. Down there wit' me other ship, Prosperity." Captain Harrington replied with misty eyes.

Jacob must have understood how much this new loss weighed heavily on his heart, as he gave his friend a tough, supporting pat on the back.

Captain Harrington drank one more swig to their health. Then he let out a stressful thought that he had been holding in for some time.

"This be my final voyage, Jacob."

Jacob's incredulous expression could be felt a mile away.

Sen-hi, who sat at the table nearest them, looked over at them with intent curiosity. She mused to herself that they looked much like two Samurai who had just come back from a raid, but, the recent silence was tense and deafening. She could only guess that the Captain had said something traumatic to cause these two boisterous men to be so quiet. She looked on, eager to find any hint as to what they were talking about, but the best she could do was watch body language and facial expressions. This is what a visiting Geisha would have to go through, no doubt, she thought.

The two "Your...final voyage? What do you mean by that, James?", Jacob probed.

"Exactly what I said. I be getting too old fer this sorta thing. The sea is a harsh..."

"A harsh mistress, yes, I know!" Jacob finished his sentence, smiling at his predictable friend.

Captain Harrington smiled back and continued,

"The government be wantin' to cut back on Oriental trade. Says there be too much risk in it. Not that I'd be agin' such an idea. Took a Samurai to get us out o' this'n, after all."

"Yes, but even though it took a Samurai, as you say, that sort of thing happens rather frequently in that part of the ocean anyway, James. It won't stop just because you retire."

"Don't ye be thinkin' that I don't be knowin' that. But at least this way I can rest assured that no more good men go to waste cause some pretty ginger boy up in New York be wantin' his spice tea or somert."

Jacob saw the resolution in his friend's eyes and decided it was best to leave this subject alone; at least for now. "So what's her story, James? Why did she come on this trip? I take it she doesn't speak English?"

The Captain laughed and motioned for Sen-hi to come over in her language. Sen-hi quickly followed his orders, glad that she was being included in their conversation, finally!

"Jacob, I'll be needin' to translate on account of the obvious." Jacob nodded in accord and the Captain asked Sen-hi several questions. Her reply sent a pleasantly anxious sensation down Jacob's spine. He had never heard a Japanese woman speak in her native tongue and this particular woman excited him because her voice was so demure and hidden, such the opposite for how she appeared.

"She said that she was sent here by Emperor May-shee, I think is his name. She was sent as an ambassador for our country. See, Japan has just won their revolution and now the royal family be the ones in power."

Jacob nodded and smiled at this new and beautiful addition to his normally uncouth surroundings.

"Really? That's interesting. So who is she supposed to meet here? I take it she wasn't originally intending to land in California. She has got to be meeting someone that speaks her language."

Jacob looked Sen-hi over again and commented, "She doesn't look like your typical...what's the word they use...Geisha?"

"All I know is we was supposed to drop her off at our port stop over yonder in ol' Mexico. But, listen here, Jacob, she said that she was told to meet someone there. He's some kind of in-betweener contact or somert from Mexico. From there, she'd be journeyin' to Virginny, methinks, so's she puts it." The Captain scratched his grizzly chin, trying to figure out this conundrum.

"Virginia? That's clear across the damned continent! How the blazes is she going to make it there?"

Sen-hi again gave her answer, a very long one this time, and the Captain responded for her to Jacob.

"This be a chore, Jacob." Jacob laughed at his friend's predicament and Sen-hi nudged him with her shoulder. When the Captain looked at her, surprised, she gave him a smirk and shook her finger at him.

"Ah! This is a smart one you have here, James! She knew you were saying something about her!"

"Oh horse puckey! Fine there, missie! Listen, Jacob, she done told me that she needs to find a way to get a letter or somert to this in-betweener feller so that he knows she is here. Then maybe he'll come and pick 'er up or they'll station her here...I put in that last part, by the by."

Jacob nodded in understanding and peered over across the street at the Processing Office.

"Well, we best be doing that then. And..." Jacob peered at Sen-hi with authority, but the seasoned warrior did not flinch. She matched his gaze for par.

"James, you can translate this if you please. Young lady, I welcome you to this fine country of ours called America. Now that you are here, though, you need to be processed and I'm afraid you shall have to turn in your weapon."

Sen-hi did not like all this news she was hearing from Captain Harrington. From what she understood, and that was second-hand information in itself, she was expected to turn over her only means of defending herself! Such a thought assailed every fiber of her being. Sen-hi was used to being treated like a woman, but this was downright insulting. She was a warrior, a Samurai, for Buddha's sake! And besides, she thought as they entered another building, she was sent as a goodwill ambassador from Japan. Surely, that must give her some sort of diplomatic immunity? Sen-hi decided one of the first things she would do in this new country is to learn the language so that she could defend herself.

"Ah, so I understand that this is a new arrival? Wonderful, another Chinaman. Come to join the Circus, have you?" The man's tone was annoyed and shallow. Sen-hi looked him over and came to the conclusion that whatever he was saying, it could not be a good thing. She stared at him with a menace in her eyes that would send shivers down any man's spine.

Captain Harrington had told her during the voyage of the growing hatred towards any Asian immigrants. The aftermath of the Barbary Coast Wars, coupled with the massive surge of immigrants from China had made the Americans, he told her, paranoid and angry.

"Jacob, does this...what do they call them, Sameray, does he have papers?", the officer asked.

"What are ye, man, blind? She be a woman!", Captain Harrington barked.

Robert, the officer, squinted at Sen-hi, as if straining to see the impossible truth that was just told to him.

"There is no possible way that this is a woman!"

Captain Harrington turned to Sen-hi as she angrily whispered a question in his ear. The old Captain sighed in frustration at the situation and relayed the answer to Sen-hi. When Sen-hi heard the insult that was being directed towards her, she immediately decided that she would hear no more nonsense from this cowardly worker.

In one stroke, Sen-hi untied her sheathed sword and brought it down on the table where Robert was sitting. Robert was so surprised at this sudden turn of events, that he did not notice his pen split in two. From the wind, the force from a sheath! Two harbor guards quickly appeared from around the back of the customs office and approached Sen-hi, their guns at the ready.

"No one took her weapon? What is this, a zoo? Miss, I'm afraid we must ask you to give your weapon to us. You were wise to leave it in its holster and I WILL overlook your blatant action, but I still must ask for you to give it to me for the time being.", one of the guards said.

"Wait! Wait! She don't understand! This is all a big misunderstandin', this is!" James tried so hard to quell the situation, but it was no use. Sen-hi was a Samurai and every Samurai knew there was to be no surrendering when confronted with an enemy. Sen-hi defiantly lifted her sheathed sword from the table and pointed it at the guards. A flicker of pride coursed through her. She knew now there was no possible way these amateur fighters with their primitive weapons could stand against the ancient Sakeda blade.

The two guards saw her pointing at them and, sheathed or not, they saw it as a provocation and started firing around Sen-hi, but she was already expecting this tactic from them. Sen-hi deftly dodged the shots and used that time to bound towards the two guards. The higher ranking guard saw her do this, took out his whistle and blew it.

The two guards nodded to each other in silent agreement as to their next tactic and stopped firing. Sen-hi jumped away from them, in the event that they threw an explosive. When she saw that they did not, she relaxed her stance somewhat.

"Sen-hi, don't fight them. They are too crafty and their weapons are too much for you. Just do what they tell you. You have my word that no harm will come to you." Sen-hi leered at her friend, Captain Harrington, the only person in this new world that spoke her language so far. The only person she could count on for support.

"They insulted my honor, Captain. They deserve death at my hands."

"It would be unwise to engage them, especially with intent to kill."

"Why is that? There are only two guards and what looks like their Captain over there near the bar." She motioned over to the man relaxed against the bar.

"There is something you are not counting on." He replied, looking over to the entrance.

Within an instant, the customs office filled with armed guards and naval officers, all called in by the Guard's whistle, just as Captain Harrington expected.

"I heard your whistle outside, Seaman, good work." The Captain looked over at Harrington and nodded, "Captain Harrington, as the highest ranking shore-bound Officer, I will take over from here. I was informed of the matter and I can speak her language relatively well." James nodded at the Harbor Captain and patted his friend, Sen-hi, on the shoulder. "I think it best you listen to this man. He is not one to trifle with." Sen-hi bowed her head in defeat and looked on reluctantly at the obvious course of action in front of her. She decided that she would hear this man out and very slowly lowered her sheathed weapon. Perhaps he would have some sense and treat her with some dignity. Even the most uncouth Japanese men treated her with better manners than these bastards. The Captain of the Guards, a Lieutenant Robert Macarthur, as the other men were referring to him, motioned for her to come forward. As she slowly, cautiously made her way over to him, four guards quickly approached her and attempted to wrest her sword from her.

Sen-hi did not cut their hands off, even though she could have, sheath and all. Instead, she merely peered at this 'Lieutenant Robert Macarthur' and motioned with her head at the four guards around her.

"No! Leave her alone, boys! I'm going to do this the smart way!" The guards immediately heeded their Captain's orders. Sen-hi got within speaking distance of the Captain and he smiled warmly. She did not return the smile.

"I see. Of course, you're not happy. I am truthfully sorry for this misunderstanding. Please permit me to be of *restaurant* service, miss." His Japanese may not have been perfect, Sen-hi mused, but it still comforted her somewhat that this man was trying to be decent towards her, especially after what she had just been through with the other barbarians. Suddenly, the enormity of the events of the past couple of months, both on board the ship and here, flooded upon her. Slowly, tears started forming in Sen-hi's eyes. She looked upon this man and tried hard to fight back the tears, but it was most difficult. This man, she thought, his voice was so comforting, that she almost thought of letting go of her sword. The Captain proceeded to take off his hat and took to one knee, with some difficulty, she realized. Sen-hi saw this act of kindness and decided to return the favor by slowly tying her sword back to her hakama, while cautiously looking around at her surroundings through tear-soaked eyes.

"What is your name?" The Captain asked in her language, while slowly getting up.

"Sen-hi Sakeda, daughter of Masatoshi Sakeda, creator of the legendary ancient blade of Sakeda-Ryu and Royal Ambassador of the Most Holy Empire of god on Earth, The Emperor Meiji, Japan."

"Well met, Sen-hi Sakeda. My name is Lieutenant Robert Macarthur. I am the standing Captain of this...er...*boat place*...and the Warden of the local San Francisco *boat place holding jail prison place*."

Sen-hi bowed in respect towards her newly acquired ally, or at least he seemed that way for now.

"I know that our ways seem...*not same* to you, but I must ask that you obey our rules."

"Captain Macarthur, I have no problem with complying with orders and rules. What I do have a problem with is that man." Captain Macarthur followed Sen-hi's arm as it pointed to Robert, the customs agent.

"What exactly did he do that made you react so savagely?"

"He spoke to me as if I were lower than dirt, even though I had stated before that I was sent here under official proclamation from His Royal Highness, Emperor Meiji, whom I serve."

"All right, all right. Calm down, Miss. May I see this proclamation?"

Sen-hi happily complied with his request. She took out the royal parchment that was entrusted to her all the way back in Japan and handed it to Lieutenant Macarthur. He carefully broke the royal seal, scanned it slowly, smiling and read it aloud for everyone, including Sen-hi, to hear.

"To the most illustrious new neighbor and ally in our cause for unity, America, and to whom this letter concerns: I do hereby give unto you this gift of friendship between our two nations. Please accept this girl as a token of my appreciation of keeping trade between our two countries open. Please disregard any notion of hers that she is an ambassador or noble or descendant of any sort of royal or noble lineage. She was one of my concubines and any weapons she may have on her persons were more than likely stolen from a soldier that she brutally murdered upon trying to escape her destiny. Please do with her what you want. She is to be regarded as you would regard a common street wench. Yours always in fervor and in faith, The Lord Emperor Meiji, Kyoto, Japan."

Every word hit Sen-hi harder than any sword strike ever could. Lieutenant Macarthur saw the look on her face and decided it was appropriate to let her see the letter for herself, even if he himself was a little surprised that a common wench could read anything. Sen-hi's eyes feverishly read over the exact same words she heard. She battled against all the demons in her head, laughing, jeering at her foolish thoughts of being a so-called wielder of an ancient blade of any sort and could not believe that it was true. All of what was read to her was right there in front of her, just staring her straight in the face and she suddenly felt alone and betrayed.

The Emperor that she swore her life to, who she was related to, the man that she spoke to with such honor and kindness before her departure so many months ago had betrayed her in a most disgusting fashion. The letter slowly left her hands and fell to the floor, along with her resolve and dignity. It was as if the Sen-hi she knew, the legendary warrior, other-worldly strength and power, noble stories her father told her, everything she came to know before crossing the great ocean, left her. She did not feel like a warrior anymore. She felt, truly, like that wench in the letter. Sen-hi looked within herself, searched for meaning but found only emptiness. "I am nothing. I have nothing. I have been betrayed."

"Miss, I know this must be difficult for you, but it is the truth. You must accept that you are no more than a gift to this country. A peace offering, if you will."

Sen-hi vehemently shook her head in protest. She was not to be a gift...to anyone! She was not to be treated like garbage. With one swift motion, she went for her sword and, to her horror, instead of the sword unsheathing, it remained in its sheath, unyielding to her grasp. No amount of strength released it. She struggled, yet it did not unsheathe. While she tried understanding this unknown force stopping her from actually using her weapon, she felt the warm hand of a man wrenching her sword from her, taking away her soul, the last bit of honor that she had in her and any evidence that she had ever been a warrior. She was now totally naked. Totally alone. Sen-hi let out a scream that echoed throughout the office.

"Soo-d! Soo-d!" She yelled, knowing that that was the word for sword after she heard the Lieutenant saying it several times to his men. Her frantic eyes landed upon Lieutenant Macarthur, who was holding her beloved sword, the soul of a Samurai Warrior. Her knees locked in paralytic shock. No one had ever successfully stolen her sword before!

"I'm afraid we cannot give you back this weapon, my dear. As you heard in the letter, you obviously stole them from..."

"It is a LIE! I stole from no one, Lieutenant! My father was Masatoshi Sakeda! He was a legendary swordsman. I am not a...a....whore! Give me back my father's sword! Your hands must not tarnish it!"

"Yes, yes, I'm sure you do not wish to be thought of as a whore, but we must believe what the Emperor says. After all, was it not you that called him 'His Highness' and that you served him with your life?" Sen-hi reluctantly nodded, but quickly shook her head in defiance of this grave news.

"Seaman, take her to the jail. Lock her there until I can ascertain what is to be done with her."

"Yes sir." The Seaman made a motion for the nearby guards to shackle her, which Sen-hi would not allow. She knew that they figured she was defenseless without her sword and she was about to show them how truly legendary her fighting style was. Before she could get her feet in the position she needed though, she felt a cold hard thud to the back of her head and then all she knew was darkness.

CHAPTER TWO
BLOOD OATH

The grass near Right Hand's hiding spot behind a tree near one of the many caves of the great Úytaahkoo Mountain swayed back and forth under the hypnotic trance of the wind. He knew that today would not be favorable for battle with arrows, yet his father's resolve was strong. They would have to fight again for their land. The white man was coming this way and neither Right Hand, nor his father knew how to barter with their type. The young Mapiyan warrior did not understand how anyone could refuse barter with his father, though, despite that. There were so many wonderful goods that could be traded, it was difficult to imagine any man that could turn them down. His father, Elder Proud Eagle, was very stern about these pale-faced devils. He often told the people of the Mapiya Nation never to venture past the Holy Stones near the mountain. "They were placed there by The Great Spirit to protect our people," He would say, "...and they are not to be passed. To do so would insult The Great Spirit's gift and provoke the presence of the white demons." Right Hand obeyed his father's wishes very clearly. He surely did not want the white man to venture into their land through the Holy Stones high in the mountains. The number of Mapiya warriors had thinned in number as of late and they would not survive another fight. Still, he sighed, a battle must be fought and today would be that day. The white men had already crossed the Holy Stones and were within a half-day of the village, where Two Moons and Loud Wolf, his friends, were waiting.

Meanwhile, closer to the village, Two Moons and his best friend and third in command of the Mapiya tribe, Loud Wolf, sat opposite him behind a large rock. The shade gave them the advantage that they sorely needed. Two Moons noticed several gestures that his friend, Loud Wolf, was making not so far from him. Two Moons grimaced at what he knew the gestures meant. He quickly un-notched his axe holster and prepared for the worst.

The first sign came in the form of two scouts. They were dressed in the usual garb, as described by the Elder. The two scouts were a good distance from each other, Two Moons thought. They did not seem to be aware of their presence. Two Moons gave the motion for Loud Wolf to stay silent and gave out a bird call. The two scouts stopped in their tracks and looked around, guns pointing wildly into the air around them. "Didja hear that, Jeb?"

"Yeah. Sounded like some sort of wild bird."

"Yeah, hey, we should head back and tell the Captain that this area looks clean. Good place to set up camp. There's even a river right straight over this ridge here."

"That ain't a river, iggit, it's a crik or something."

"Well, whatever it is, it's water."

Two Moons slowly followed one of the scouts' arms as he seemed to point at the sacred spring that the Mapiyans used as their primary source of water.

Two Moons knew now that these two men had to be killed. They had traversed the mountain trail and crossed the Holy Stones, pointing their foreign fingers towards the sacred waters. Just as Two Moons was about to give the order to attack, though, the scouts turned around and rode back. He fell back down on his position and waited for the right moment before him and Loud Wolf returned to their village.

Sen-hi abruptly awoke to the sounds of clanging and screams of pain. She looked around and noticed that she was in a jail cell. The cell stunk of old dry urine and droppings from the other prisoners that had been in this place before her. She could not believe this was happening. She attempted to lift her hands to rub the sleep off of her eyes and could not lift them. Instead, she heard the unmistakable sound of chains rattling again. She peered down and saw that she was shackled to the wall behind her, rather tightly at that. She also noticed that her traditional clothes had been replaced by a smelly and stained long shirt which had a frayed rope tied around its center. The noises of loud footsteps brought her eyes to the entrance of her cell, a large rusted cell door, bolted shut. She could see in between the bars fine enough, but her vision was impaired due to the extreme darkness that invaded the hallway. 'What madmen are trapped in such a god-forsaken place?', she thought. She remembered Captain Macarthur and how nice he was to her and then looked again at her surroundings. Her eyes met the floor beneath her. It was littered with old hay and a rusted bowl, no doubt used for food. 'Did he deceive me?' She wondered. It was the only thing that made sense. She had never met any Americans before, but she was quickly starting to dislike them intensely. Sen-hi then decided that the best thing to do was not to focus on the past. 'I have to find a way out of here. Back to Japan. Back to revenge.' She looked at her feet and studied the shackles. They hurt very badly and whoever put them on obviously did not care to attend to whether they were too tight or not, for she tried to move them up and down, yet they would not budge. Sen-hi attempted to walk around the cell and she noticed that the closer she got to the cell door, the harder it was for her to keep going. 'Is this some kind of magic?' She struggled with all of her might to grab hold of the iron bars, yet within an inch of grasping them, she was violently pulled backwards and slammed against the back wall. The shock was so severe, that it knocked her unconscious.

Elder Proud Eagle furrowed his brow at the dire news that Two Moons brought before the council. The white man had come beyond the sacred threshold and had pointed with his white arm at the sacred spring.

"You are certain that there were only two scouts, Two Moons?" The Elder asked.

"Elder, I am most certain that there were only two. However, upon returning to our home, I asked Sister Eagle if she saw any others approaching our home, and she told me that there was a large group heading towards the sacred waters from across the forest."

"Did she specify whether she felt they would continue to head east towards us?"

"No, Elder. She flew off before I could ask her any more."

"I see. Then we must do our part. We must defend the sacred water at all costs. If the white man touches it, he will surely desecrate it."

"Of that, you can be certain!" Spirit Bear, the tribe's Shaman, belted out, shaking his staff.

"Medicine Man, I will speak with you in more detail in private. Leave us, my brothers. Attend to your women and children. Warn them of the impending battle and prepare. This will not be an easily won victory." The council members agreed to Elder Proud Eagle's suggestion.

Back in Proud Eagle's tent, Spirit Bear was sitting, awaiting more instructions from Proud Eagle. He was very proud to be in the same tent as his good friend. When he was younger, Proud Eagle was named "Willing Ox" for his eagerness to do good deeds for others, regardless of the burdens that were placed upon him. Spirit Bear was there for the ceremony that assigned the title "Fire Owner" to Proud Eagle, given to him after the battle with the white eye miners. Many of his brethren had been killed nearly to extinction by the filthy, greedy miners in their search for the golden rocks. The white eye polluted the precious waters across the land of his fathers, killing millions of fish, a major food source for his people. This is why they needed a strong voice in the council of tribes for the Mapiya. There were no real leaders among the tribe, only a council of elders and Proud Eagle had always been the main voice of reason within the council. It was why so many elders listened and adhered to his words. Yes, Spirit Bear, thought, albeit an odd behavior for Mapiya people, the council voted as one, and that vote almost always was influenced by Proud Eagle's words.

It could not be denied that Proud Eagle was the greatest Elder that the Mapiya people ever had. Spirit Bear had never seen his friend back down from a challenge, let alone get anxious over an upcoming battle. The Shaman was about to learn, though, that all things change eventually.

"Old friend, I have to admit that I am quite worried about this." Proud Eagle said, entering his tent and sitting across from his friend, Spirit Bear.

"Worried? You? Don't be silly, my friend. You will vanquish these white demons. Of that, I am sure!" The Medicine Man patted the Elder's back, but it did not console the old leader. Instead, Proud Eagle shook his head and looked his friend in the eyes.

"Brother Spirit Bear, I have spoken to survivors of the Red Plains Massacre."

The Shaman blanched with fear. He had heard of that atrocious attack. It was aptly named a massacre. The white devils killed everyone, including the children.

"I thought none had escaped that barbarity."

"It seems that The Great Spirit was merciful to our brothers and sisters. Some managed to escape the attack. This brings me to my next point. I do not think we can outnumber the soldiers."

"Surely you are in jest, old friend. You heard Two Moons, they sent only two scouts!"

"They were only scouts, Spirit Bear. You have heard the stories of the white throngs blanketing the land, staining it with unholy feet."

Spirit Bear waved his hand, dismissing the elder's cryptic description. "They are but myths. There cannot be such a force of men. Think of it, how is it that they could have amassed such a fighting force in such a small amount of time, friend?"

"Some say they came in large canoe ships capable of carrying hundreds of men. Some say that they came across the great waters."

"The End of the Earth? Not possible! No man could survive such a trek, you know that!"

Spirit Bear saw his friend's look of concern and understood it. His people were limited in their views of the world around them. They lived in the mountains, after all, and had never had any contact with foreigners. The news of several Mapiyan deaths near the foothills troubled him greatly. Not all of those deaths could be from falling off the mountainside, after all. When Two Moons and Loud Wolf told the council that the white man was stabbing the mountainside in search of golden rocks last year, he knew that their time had come.

"There are times, Spirit Bear, that I fear for the weakness of the council members."

"Elder?" Spirit Bear uttered, barely able to understand this new behavior emanating from his friend.

"Do not misunderstand me, old friend. I do not doubt the ability of my fellow Elders, nor have I lost faith in our overall decisions. I am speaking of what we can do as a group. I am sure that it is only my weak mind that is conjuring these dark thoughts, though. Please, friend, give me some medicine so that I may wake myself from this dark dream."

"In dreams, sometimes we find darkness that leads to light." Spirit Bear suggested, casting a fine white powder in front of Proud Eagle and shaking his staff over his friend's head. Within seconds, the Elder fell into a deep sleep.

Proud Eagle suddenly found himself in the middle of the sacred river. Its strong current was pulling on his thick legs, but, strangely, he was not being taken away. Across the water, his son, Right Hand, was standing looking at him and yelling something. Proud Eagle strained to hear the words. Instead, he heard a loud rushing sound, like that of a waterfall crashing over the side of a cliff. Suddenly, a salmon swam up to his leg and poked its head out of the water. Amazingly, the words that his son was yelling came to him through the lips of that very salmon. "Father! The one with the crossed eye will be chosen!"

"What does that mean, Brother Salmon?"

The fish only repeated the answer again, "The one with the crossed eye will be chosen."

In the flash of an instant, the Salmon grew and turned into a large knife, the likes of which he had never seen. It looked like a type of saber, like the kind he often saw the white eye wear, however, this one was curved and had a strange square-shaped hilt. Just as Proud Eagle had studied this odd instrument, it leapt from the water and flew across the river and plunged right into his son's heart! Proud Eagle tried with all his might to get to his son first, but the current was too strong. "It is destiny, Father. You cannot change it." Right Hand collapsed on the river bed, drenched in blood. Proud Eagle cried aloud for The Great Spirit's help, but he received no answer. Instead, he witnessed another spectacle. Beyond the river bed, almost to the very horizon, Proud Eagle saw a massive army marching towards him and the river. Their armor was so bright, that it reflected off of the shimmering water. Proud Eagle marveled at the speed of this great force. As the group got closer, His last vision was that of the face of his new enemy. He noticed to his horror that it was not their armor that was shining, it was their faces. In the blink of an eye, the army raised their odd stick weapons and, with a loud bang, louder than any thunder he had ever heard, Proud Eagle saw no more.

Lieutenant Macarthur's office was an absolute mess. He had promised himself that he would clean it, but, he did not count on being away for so long. It had been three months since he had been in Monterey and dealt with a very unusual situation involving a Japanese... or Chinese...prostitute who apparently bartered, stole and, more than likely, killed her way to get to America and he was hoping he would not have to deal with any situations like that anymore. Now, he was back in San Francisco bay and he was being told by his commanding officer who had received several letters from a Captain Harrington that the same girl he had sent to jail had been demanding to see him.

"James has been coming in to see her?" Macarthur's commanding officer inquired as he shuffled several old papers into a drawer and offered his Commanding Officer a seat. Macarthur remained standing, a common procedure. The commanding officer wore his displeasure at Macarthur's mess of an office very visibly. The Lieutenant cursed himself quietly for not ordering someone to take care of the desk for him.

"I was just as surprised as you are, Captain, but it is the truth. She has had two regular visitors. Captain James Harrington and Jacob Miller, the Harbor Master." Commanding Officer Captain Lance Stephens nodded, tracing a finger across the rim of Macarthur's desk and looking closely at it.

"I don't understand, sir." Macarthur said, trying hard not to notice his Superior Officer's displeasure, "Why would a whore like her have any visitors?"

"Perhaps she is not, as you say, a whore, Robert."

"Sir, it cannot be denied that she is so. Her letter, after all, stated that she…"

"I am aware of the letter, Lieutenant. I read it in detail. During your absence, I spoke with several Japanese immigrants about the current situation in their country."

"But what of it, sir? What do they have to do with the girl?"

"Well, apparently, there had been rumors of a plot against her and some other samurai that had been close to her. They said that the very Emperor himself, that these samurai practically placed in power, sent her over here in the hopes that she would be killed."

"That can be arranged, I assure you." Macarthur commented with a sneer.

Captain Stevens looked the Lieutenant over and was taken aback by this statement. "Robert, at ease."

"Sir. Thank you, sir."

"You have permission to speak freely, Robert."

"Thank you, Sir."

"First, would you please close the door?", Stephens asked, Macarthur quickly complying. "Why are you so quick to kill this girl? Has she done something harsh to you…or one of your men?" Stephens put forth, slowly placing the letters from Captain Harrington inside his front pocket.

"No sir, certainly not. She's…she's a whore sir, quite frankly, and I have no place in my jail for someone like that."

"What do you mean, 'someone like that'?"

"A sinner of the worst kind, sir."

"Worst kind?" Stephens balked at this response. He had never known Macarthur as well as he would have liked, but he surely had never heard talk like this from any of his men. "Go on."

"Sir, I am a Christian and a Soldier. I joined this Soldier's Army because I wanted to help my country spread the good news throughout the land and fight for what's right, by whatever means necessary, Sir. The President may be my Commander-In-Chief, but the Bible is my one and only guide to living and protecting."

"Yes, that's all well and good, but that still doesn't answer my question of why her being a prostitute bothers you so?"

"The Bible is very clear about whores, sir. They are to be stoned and cleansed of sin. They have no place among decent, God-fearing Christians, like you and I, sir."

"Lieutenant, I am not like you. I keep my religion and my career separate."

Macarthur uncomfortably leered at his Commander. He felt very awkward. "Permission to leave, sir."

"Permission denied, Lieutenant. You'll have to learn to live with and take orders from someone that is not an...say, you're one of those Evangelist Christians, aren't you?"

Macarthur nodded emphatically. "Christ above...stand at attention, Soldier." Macarthur immediately composed himself and stood erect, ready to take the next order. Stephens grumbled, "Macarthur, let me see this girl." Macarthur reluctantly opened the door and proceeded to escort his superior officer to the cells below.

Upon arriving in the hallway where Sen-hi was being held, Stephens had to put a tissue to his nose, to cover the awful stench that was emanating from the corridor. His eyes furiously scanned both sides of the jail, trying to reason out the atrocious conditions of this place.

"What kinds of prisoners are kept in this corridor, Lieutenant?"

"The most despicable and offensive types, sir." Macarthur immediately answered, motioning to the last cell in the corridor.

"And you placed her down here? What crime has she committed that she was to be sent down here, Lieutenant?"

"Sir, she attempted to kill my men and she lied..."

"Lieutenant Macarthur..." Stephens interrupted, facing him head on, "...are you trying to tell me that you locked her up down in this hellhole with these other miscreants on the charge of attempted murder?"

Macarthur looked his superior officer square in the eyes and responded, "I would have done worse by now if you hadn't shown up, sir."

Stephens was greatly troubled by this statement and it showed. He fervently ordered Macarthur to open the door and let him in, despite Macarthur's incessant nagging to the contrary. Stephens slowly made his way into the dark cell and was appalled at the grotesque nature of what was before him. He was even more appalled when he saw the lanky, pale human being staring back at him, hanging upon the wall, connected to it with shackles on her hands and feet. The chains on the shackles ran the length of the room, connected to a gear and pulley system, recently put in place by the Military to discourage escape. If the inmate were to walk too close to the doors of the cell, the gears would click into action and fling the prisoner back to their prison on the wall. Yet beyond the stench and decay surrounding her, Stephens could not ignore a beauty hidden beyond her dirty face. He was truly enraptured. He decided then and there that he would have to learn more about this trapped flower.

"Lieutenant, did the prisoner ever...mention a name?"

"I only translated what I had to, Sir, I..."

"Macarthur! I asked you a question! Did she mention her family name or, more importantly, her fighting style? You know Japanese, you should know!"

Captain Macarthur shook visibly in anger and reluctantly answered, "She said her name was 'Sen-hi Sakeda', sir."

Captain Stephens' eyes widened in shock. "It can't be. Not...this is impossible."

"What is, sir, that I haven't killed her yet? I agree fully."

"Get her down immediately, Lieutenant!" Stephens barked, pointing at Sen-hi, who was still chained to the back wall of the cell.

"We placed her in this type of cell, sir, also because she is an accomplished warrior and we wanted to make sure that..."

"That's enough! I will hear no more nonsense from you! You are to carry this poor woman out of here and bring my carriage to meet me out front. I am now in charge of her and will take full responsibility for her well-being, a task which, I see, was too great for you, Lieutenant Macarthur!"

Macarthur was speechless. His bottom lip was quivering with rage. He wanted to scream out at Captain Lance Stephens, but he realized that, unfortunately, he was not in a position to do so...at least not yet. He felt that he had done the right thing in putting this whore in jail. He felt that, perhaps, he had made an example of her in public and that maybe others like her would choose a life of chastity instead of the sinful life she chose. Macarthur unlocked Sen-hi's shackles and violently scooped up her up in his arms as ordered and made his way to the front of the jail accompanied by his Captain. He revolted at the smell of urine that emanated from her clothing. *No doubt she defecated on herself as well*, he thought. He always hated that he learned their barbaric language and kept reminding himself that the only reason he learned it was that one day, he would be stationed in Japan to help eliminate them, as he was sure that was what the forces sent to Japan years ago were doing even now.

The horses trotted to the entrance of the harbor's jail and Stephens took Sen-hi from the Lieutenant and gently placed her in his carriage. Normally a clean man, Captain Lance Stephens did not care to place a towel or tissue on the seat. *Perhaps we are the true heathens*, Stephens thought. "You are dismissed from your duties in this jail, Lieutenant Macarthur and should expect a re-assignment and letter of reprimand from me regarding this disgusting and inhumane action upon my arrival at our headquarters. Good day, Lieutenant." Stephens immediately slammed the door of the carriage and gave the motion for his driver to head to his home and headquarters further inland, leaving behind him an enraged Lieutenant Macarthur.

"You may think this is over, Captain," the Lieutenant whispered to himself as the carriage was rolling away, "One day I will have my revenge against that bitch and you will understand why I believe the way I do and why that is the right way."

CHAPTER THREE

RIGHTS OF PASSAGE

The dark, damp cave on the side of the mountain gave little shelter to Jack and Bill. They knew it was risky to travel up-river, but the "gold fever" had gotten a hold of them and, as far as they were concerned, they were going to find those shiny nuggets.

"Do ya think that we'll run into any other diggers up here, Bill?"

"Doubt we'll run into some live ones. There've been lots of prospectors caught up here dead as dirt."

"Whoda thought that there were injuns up here too? It's clear up to heaven, this mountain!"

"I know. Still, we best be careful."

The two miners picked away at the inside of the mountain, hoping to hear that special sound that meant that they found something. Even though many miners had lost their lives in this mountain, they were determined to find some gold. But just as their search began, so too did it end. The two miners did not realize that a Mapiyan warrior was among them, but cloaked in darkness. Within a fraction of a second, an arrow shot through the darkness and impaled Bill straight through his throat. Jack watched in horror as his friend collapsed to the floor, choking on his own blood. Fearing for his own life, he threw down his pickaxe and darted towards the entrance of the cave, only to be met by the savage that killed his friend. "You bastard! You kilt my friend!" Jack quickly brandished his rusty knife and waved it madly in the air, thinking to scare this barbarian off.

Just as the young warrior ran towards him, a loud thundering bang stopped him in his tracks. Jack's eyes lit up with relief when he looked up and saw his savior at the mouth of the cave holding a smoking gun in his quivering hand.

The Mapiyan warrior, Loud Wolf by name, looked behind at his murderer and memorized the insignia on the man's upper arm. As Jack ran out of the cave, following his friend, in disbelief of his luck, Loud Wolf did the only thing he could think of. As he lay dying slowly of a bullet wound in the chest, Loud Wolf grabbed the other miner's pickaxe, soaked it in his own blood and started to work on the cavern floor.

Sen-hi's eyes slowly opened after being closed for an unknown amount of time. She arose and took in her surroundings, trying very hard not to make any noise. She was laying in a bed made of the softest, most wonderful material she had ever felt. It had to be silk. She also realized that she was wearing a very comfortable kimono. Sen-hi felt her face and noticed that, not only was it clean, but the scars had almost completely disappeared! She quickly grabbed a nearby hand mirror and brought it before her. Her hair was not matted, dirty or unkempt and she felt rested. At once she thought that she had perhaps died in that cell and had achieved Nirvana, but she knew that this could not be true paradise. She decided that she would get out of bed and try to ascertain her location. However, upon her descent, the door to her room swiftly opened and Sen-hi fell back onto her bed, making as if she were still asleep. A jolly, dark-skinned woman entered the room, carrying what looked like linens and some other ceramic urns and containers which Sen-hi had never seen before.

"Now, Miss Sunny, are we gonna be good today, or is I goin' ta have ta get my boxin' gloves?"

Sen-hi did not understand the woman at all, but she figured that this dark woman must be a servant of some sort, for she was wearing a patterned dress that Sen-hi supposed was a servant's uniform. She merely shrugged at the woman, hoping that she would understand that.

"Oh, Miss Sunny, I know you can't understand me, sugar. I am Miss Anne. Can you say my name, baby? Miss....Anne." The dark woman kept patting her chest and repeating the same two words which Sen-hi took as her name. She slowly mouthed the words, "Mees....Ahn." and pointed at the woman. "Close enough, Miss Sunny. Do you know that is your name? Sunny." Miss Anne pointed at Sen-hi and said "Sunny" repetitively. Sen-hi rolled her eyes at the mispronunciation of her name but tolerated it, figuring that it would be probably be difficult to teach these barbarians how her name was truly pronounced.

"Now, I know that you can't understand me, Miss Sunny, but I'm your caretaker here at Master Stephens' house. The war has been over for many years, but he pays me well for my services and my babies are good and fed, I can't complain. Master Stephens, he be the one that got you out of jail, you see." Sen-hi paid close attention to Miss Anne's mouth movements, intonation and manner of speech as the dark woman placed all the ceramic containers in a table in front of her. Sen-hi pointed at the containers and shrugged her shoulders. Miss Anne gave a warm smile and said, "We're gonna fix you up real pretty for Mr. Stephens, sugar. He's havin' company over later today and he wants to show you off to the General. Word around here is, you might be workin' with me pretty soon. Course I gon' havta lurn you English, Sunny, now isn't I?" Sen-hi winced as Miss Anne splashed cold water on her face. In several minutes, Miss Anne dressed Sen-hi and walked her to the large mirror in her room. She looked at her reflection and blanched. The woman staring back at her was unfamiliar. The reflection was decorated with shiny baubles and wore a long, fat dress. It wasn't until Sen-hi touched her self that she realized she really was the woman in the mirror. She wanted to cry out in protest, but Miss Anne put a hand to her mouth. "Now, don't fuss, girl. Master Stephens went through a lot to get you cleared of your charges and the only thing he asks is for you to wear this and smile and act nice and all to his guests. You think you can do that?" Sen-hi did not understand her caretaker's words, but she guessed that she was telling her to behave. She reluctantly nodded and gave her hand to Miss Anne. "All right, let's go meet that Captain of ours."

Proud Eagle could not believe his eyes. In front of him, right in front of him and inside the tent of the Elders, lie a dead Mapiya warrior, massacred to death by two ignorant miners. He had thought, perhaps, by sending Loud Wolf to the cave he could acquire some clues to the mystery of the encroachers' motives, but the dark red blood stained on his nephew's chest pulsed through his clarity and served as motive enough. These people were not peacemakers. They were the bringers of death. Yet even people such as these, Proud Eagle thought, may still be reasoned with. "We must find a way to speak with one of their leaders, my brethren." Proud Eagle put forth, standing within the circle. The other elders looked up at him and he could see the desperation in their eyes. They always looked at him like that when they were lost. They needed an answer, and Proud Eagle did not have one right now. "It is true that they have killed my nephew, our brother, Loud Wolf. But it is not for us to decide who lives or dies. We must go to them and speak with them. Perhaps they have already tried and sentenced these men? Surely, murder is not a soft crime in their world."

"Elder Eagle, pray, allow that I may lend some advice herein."

The council's attention shifted to one particular location in the circle, that of Elder Right Hand. "Speak, Right Hand, for it is not the purpose of this councilmember to usurp any authority." Proud Eagle humbly made his way to his seat in the council and gave the floor, rather reluctantly, to Right Hand. The youngest of all the Elders, Right Hand's ideas were always thought of as controversial and against the tribe's edicts. Proud Eagle knew, however, that this event that transpired may have clouded the minds of the council; and that he knew, may prove to be deadly in the young elder's hands.

"Brethren, these white demons have invaded our land. They have killed one of our own. These are violations of all we stand for, are they not?" The council members all vigorously nodded their heads, awaiting the next words from their young, vibrant member.

"For many long years we have been led, as a group, by the boisterous and pleasant words of Elder Proud Eagle, however, these are not times for pleasantries. These are times for action!" Right Hand thrust his right hand in the air, a habit that had earned him his name. The council erupted into emphatic cries of "Death to the encroachers!" "Right Hand is our true voice!" "Blood has been spilled!". Right Hand's contented smile went unnoticed in the raucous jubilation by all but one member. Proud Eagle's eyes met that of Right Hand's and the warriors stayed staring at each other in that room, knowing full well what the other was thinking. Proud Eagle swore he would discover the true nature of his son's course of action. He swore that he would find a diplomatic course of action against the intruders. Even if it killed him.

Captain Lance Stephens marveled at the work that Anne did on the Asian girl. He was so enamored at the sight of her, that he left the Mayor standing by himself in the reception room of his house, just to go over and see her. "My dear, you look absolutely breathtaking." Stephens barely uttered, slowly taking her hand and bringing it up to his lips to kiss it. Sen-hi quickly recoiled, bouncing into Miss Anne's stocky body. "Miss Anne, have you informed this girl that I am her caretaker now?" "Yessah, but I's don't know how good she can understand me, Suh. I don't even know what talk she know?"

"So be it, Miss Anne. You and I will teach her our language. I have taught countless ignorant foreigners the Queen's English and I shall teach this girl and she will think me better for it." Stephens added the last part, enunciating each syllable while being at Sen-hi's face level.

"Bet..tur...forew...it." Sen-hi bravely repeated, looking at Stephens with contempt and pride. "Miss Anne, please take her to my quarters." Miss Anne knew what that meant for the girl. "Take her...?" "Yes, Miss Anne, or do you forget your place here?" Stephens' eyes flickered with authority. "You are to bring this girl to my quarters post haste. I need to teach her a lesson in obedience. Do I make myself clear, Miss Anne?" "Crystal, Suh." Miss Anne quickly pulled Sen-hi along behind her. Sen-hi did not know what was going on, but she was sure that this man was the "Steebens" that Miss Anne was talking about. If he was the owner of this house and, if she was thinking correctly, Miss Anne was just ordered to take Sen-hi back to her room. Once they passed her room, though, Sen-hi now knew something was very wrong. She saw the long hallway in front of her and the large double doors that inhabited the end of the hallway and could only guess at who opened those doors every night. Sen-hi pulled back at Miss Anne gently, but with purpose, and Miss Anne reluctantly stopped and looked at Sen-hi. "What is it, child? I gots to take ya to the Master's room. He be wantin' to speak wit ya." "No, Mees Ahn." Sen-hi shook her head, pointing to the double doors. "Oh, child, don't you understand that I can't say no to our master?" Sen-hi did not understand her at all, but kept repeating the same three words over and over. Miss Anne had no recourse but to forcefully, yet even more reluctantly, pull Sen-hi inside the double doors. Sen-hi's fears were realized when she saw the huge bed in the room and the whip gently placed on the mantle next to it. "NO!! Mees Ahn! NOO! Sunny No!! Soood! Soood!" "Well, now, I don't know what 'sood' means, baby, but I can't listen to you, sugah. I have to listen to Master Stephens or I get a whoopin' with that." Sen-hi followed Miss Anne's arm to the whip on the mantle and knew what would happen to her mistress if she did not comply. She agreed to behaving and patted Miss Anne on the face. "Mees Ahn. Sunny yes. Sunny yes."

"Good girl. You lurnin' already!"

Captain Stephens studied the report from the Mayor's office with great interest. There had been another incident near the caves of the Upper Messiah Mountain Range. Two miners from the nearby village of Los Palos were assaulted and almost killed by a young Indian savage, but not before one of the miners' friends were killed by the Indian. He had heard the story many times before and this time was no different. He gave the report back to his corporal who had delivered the report and looked him square in the eyes.

"Corporal, we must watch these people carefully. If they do anything else, if there are any more deaths, we must act appropriately. Post lookouts near the cave and have a scout map their terrain and report back to me. Also, dispatch a messenger to General Thomas Nelson. Inform him that I have received this message from the Mayor of Los Palos, dispatched the appropriate guards and scouts to the territory and that I humbly await further orders." The Corporal saluted his CO and quickly marched to his horse outside to deliver Stephens' message.

Sen-hi surveyed the Captain's quarters and memorized where everything was. He lived an opulent life, she thought. The table where the mirror was held all sorts of bottles that were filled of rum, liquor or some sort of perfume. She looked at the whip on the mantle and carefully picked it up, thinking through her next moves carefully. But in that instance, the door opened and Stephens himself walked in, very casually too, Sen-hi noted. In one swift motion, she cracked the whip and swung it towards Stephens, the whip snaking around his waist. Stephens did not seem surprised by this and simply took out two shuriken from out of nowhere and flicked two towards Sen-hi's hand. She instinctively dropped the whip so as to catch the ninja weapons in mid flight. Stephens then took the opportunity and deftly picked up the whip from the floor as Sen-hi grasped for the flying stars. She did not, though, and instead dodged at the last minute… right into Stephen's awaiting arms. He quickly tied her up with the whip and sat her on the bed. Sen-hi was no amateur though. She made quick work of the crude knot that he fashioned and freed herself. Within a moment she leapt to the other side of the room and snatched a sword that was hanging foolishly on the wall above his mantle.

Stephens laughed, "If you will not respect me by diplomatic means, then I will teach you to respect me through force!" Stephens quickly banged the wall behind him and a secret hatch popped open. Inside were two beautiful Samurai swords! He threw one of them at her and she caught it, dropping the inferior foreign sword. Sen-hi could not believe what she was seeing.

It was not hers, she was sure. But how could such a man possess this? Sen-hi swore she would rip it from his cold dead hands, but not before she found out how the heathen came into possession of the sword. She positioned herself, waiting for his pathetic attack and she was taken by surprise again when she saw an unbelievable sight. This man was also positioning himself in a stance similar to hers… no…it could not be. She knew that only one other man was taught the legendary Sakeda Ryu sword technique and she had killed him. Nevertheless, she decided, she would let his sword tell her where his true skill resided.

The two swords rang with a beautiful sword-song that filled the room. The warriors were so skilled that no furniture was touched, nothing was out of place. Sen-hi attempted every technique that she knew and none of them got through the insurmountable defense that this foreigner had created for her. The Mantu Ryu Sen even the Shin no Ken, her ultimate attack, were no match for Stephens' barrage of well-placed blocks, swift dodges and parries. Sen-hi also noticed that her opponent made no attempt at cutting her. Could he be tiring me out, she wondered. But before she could think any more, Stephens knocked the sword out of her hands with a devastatingly fast strike and it impaled itself against the wall on the opposite end of the room. Sen-hi sunk to the floor, defeated, ashamed and, what was worse, she lacked a short blade so as to commit seppuku. Instead, she grabbed a shuriken from the floor and attempted to slice her neck open, but the shuriken was struck away by Stephens' blade. Sen-hi looked up at her conqueror and tears of sadness, hatred and vengeance flooded her face…until she understood him speak. The tears were then replaced by eyes filled with absolute loathing.

"You have no honor if you are to end your life with such a cowardly weapon. And you have no cause to hate me, Sunny. I could have killed you but I have spared your life. The least you could do is thank me."

"You…you…understand…you speak my language? Why? How? How did you know my father's technique?"

"You mean Sakeda Ryu? I learned it from some penniless old hermit that I stumbled across in the forests of Ikeda-Haji. He said his name was Masotoshi Sakeda and that…" Stephens finally realized with whom he was speaking and stopped short of going any further. It was of no matter at any rate. The girl had something to say.

"STOP IT! STOP IT, STOP IT, STOP IT! You are lying! My father would never teach our style to a Gaijin! He would never teach it to you!"

Stephens completely understood this girl's hatred for him. He had just bested her in swordplay. Stephens thought the only fair thing to do was to tell her the whole story. He motioned for her to sit down and she reluctantly, slowly, sat on a chair. Only, though, because she wanted to know how he came to learn the sacred technique so that she could kill him. Stephens pulled up another chair and began his tale.

"About seven years ago, I was a Sailor in the Navy, aboard a ship called the "Great Fortune". My Captain, Matthias Fuller, was a great man, He was of rather stocky build with a manly Van Dyke beard, bright blue eyes and dark red hair…but he had ambitions…lust for power…which, as you know, Sunny, corrupts absolutely. Fuller, received a communiqué from his Commanding Officer to embark for the small archipelago of Japan and set up a small station there to guard the Catholic Jesuits who had missions nearby. Fuller gathered 40 of his best men and made me Pilot of the Great Fortune. I was eager to visit your island, Sunny, as I had heard much of the Samurai and the Geisha. I wanted to see these things for myself." Stephens grumbled and let out a frustrated sigh as he noticed the disbelief in Sen-hi's eyes. He knew that this girl was not going to believe his outrageous story. He then realized that the only thing for it was to tell the absolute truth about himself. After all, he needed her to know that he was the best thing she could have to a friend in this foreign land.

"The truth is, Sunny, that I have been trained in the ancient art of copy by one of your Ninjas when I visited your country those many years ago. I can watch anyone fight for any length of time and copy their moves, techniques and strategies to almost perfect accuracy. True, I really never met your father, but I did not need to. I saw a man take on a slew of ninjas that raided the village we were protecting, and he single-handedly defeated them all with ungodly power. All I needed was to watch him and I had all the knowledge I needed. So, when I noticed which position you put yourself in with your first attack, I knew your style was the same as his, what luck of providence! I later learned from a Samurai there, Toshiro, I believe was his name, that the fighting style that man used was an ancient sword fighting style called 'Sakeda Ryu', taught by a man named Masatoshi Sakeda. That is the truth."

Sen-hi trembled upon hearing Stephens's story and how he learned her style. The thought of someone else learning the ancient Sakeda blade, and by just witnessing it, revolted her. She did not understand how and why that Samurai, who must have been Akushin, would have allowed his presence to be seen, let alone copied by this man, Stephens, but she swore she would learn everything she could about this man…and then she would kill him.

"Stop it, you bastard!" Sen-hi screamed at the top of her lungs, her voice bouncing off the walls. "How dare you mention the name of my sword style in such a…such an offensive and blasphemous way? Haven't you people done enough to me, subjected me to enough torture and humiliation and now you have to slander the good name of my father who risked his life for our country? For me?"

"A country that has betrayed both of you, Sunny?" Stephens held aloft the letter that Sen-hi brought and continued, "They sent you over here with a letter stating very clearly that you are a murderer and a liar, as well as a whore. The Emperor himself sealed the letter. Are you telling me that I should not believe him? If so, are not you the one who is treasonous and blasphemous?"

Sen-hi clenched her fists in anger. Words could not express the betrayal she felt from her Emperor that she helped rise to power. Now this Gaijin...this disgusting foreigner was telling her that everything she knew was a lie. That she was not a Princess, just a simple girl from Ikeda-haji. Through her tears, she considered the weight of that title that she wore up until now. She had never truly wanted to be a Princess, she had never been trained in the ways of royalty. The only life she had ever known was that of a lowly peasant girl working tables with her sister, Megumi.

It wasn't until she joined Toshiro Mikohi's band of Samurai and assisted them in a full revolution against the Shogun Tokugawa Ieyasu and his General, Akushin Hiruma, that she finally met who she would consider her true father for the first time, even if he merely assumed that role for her protection. He revealed to her that she was really the daughter of the royal family, that he had spirited her away at a young age to protect her from the Shogun's forces. Masatoshi Sakeda raised her as his own daughter in the secluded village of Ikeda-Haji, teaching her the ways of the ancient blade of Sakeda and her world was perfect and peaceful until one of his students betrayed him and threw her world upside down.

Sen-hi composed herself as best as she could and dried her tears with her sleeve. She got up from the chair and stood facing Stephens.

"Stephens. Captain Stephens, if that is your rank, the fact of the matter is, you have defeated me. As a Samurai, I am bound by my honor to serve you as my new Master, but make no mistake, if you anger me or make me doubt you in any way, I shall cut you down and I assure you, it will be so fast, you will have no time to 'copy' anything."

Right Hand watched in detached amusement as the Spirit Fire Dance ran its course around the tribal fire in front of him. The rest of the Elders were completely entranced by the masked dancers and licks of flames that leapt to life from the ball of fire.

Right Hand never really understood why the elders put so much emphasis behind these rituals but he did understand that the tribe needed the dances so as to strengthen their connection with the Great Spirit. As expected, Right Hand's closest friend Two Moons sidled up next to him.

"May we speak, Elder Right Hand?"

"Calm yourself, brother. You know you need not call me that here. What news do you bring?"

"Our brothers at the base of the Great Valley spotted many bound horses and carriages near the border of the river. Many white men in uniform were also spotted in a nearby fort."

"They are mobilizing.", Right Hand surmised.

"That would be an astute assertion, Elder."

Right Hand sighed, but not at his friend's formality. "Two Moons, we need to mobilize as well. Get together five squads of our best warriors and meet me at the stables by the rise of the Great Circle tomorrow."

"Are we going to attack them, Elder?"

Right Hand responded with a sly smirk. "We're going to bring the fight to them before they make matters worse."

"Won't the other Elders oppose that kind of rash action?"

"The other Elders won't need to know about it, Two Moons."

"But, Right Hand, we have to..."

"Enough, Two Moons! I, Elder Right Hand, have spoken. Amass the troops. Tomorrow we meet victory or we meet death."

Two Moons nodded in confirmation and left his friend's presence. Right Hand turned his attention back to the Fire Dance. The dancing figures were now burning a passionate picture in his mind. Now they were painting a different vision. War.

Sen-hi slowly picked apart her food with the crude metal accessories that Captain Stephens had given her. These "fork and knife", as he called them, were a great deal more difficult than the sticks that she normally used to eat with. Captain Stephens insisted on her using them, though. He assured her that these utensils were much more civilized and would make eating easier and cleaner. Sen-hi could not see the logic in it, but she allowed him this small victory. The white man's food was bland and lacked taste or color. She struggled to chew the beef and wondered what kind of meat it was. Captain Stephens' loud footfalls became more prominent and, finally, the chair opposite Sen-hi gave way to the Captain's massive form. She had to admit to herself that he was an amazing figure of a man. Captain Lance Stephens, she thought, must have been molded by Buddha himself. He had wide, broad shoulders, a face that seemed to be made for having a beard, yet had not yet discovered the need for it, and a chest that just poured beautifully into the pristine uniform. And his eyes. Sen-hi glanced somewhat whimsically at the Captain's endless green eyes and hated herself for it. They sparkled in the low light hue of the house's dining room, much like the stars over Ikeda-haji during the twilight hours. Stephens slapped his full plate down with the efficiency and professionalism of a soldier. Sen-hi noted with some amusement at how all of his servings were perfectly divided on the plate. No part of any of the food touched the other. He seemed to feel her gaze and slowly lifted his head to meet her eyes. "I apologize if I startled you. I am in a bit of a fever." Sen-hi did not understand what he meant by the Kanji for fever, however, she could see the frustration quite plainly on his face. "So, did Miss Anne feed you?"

"Yes." Sen-hi stated, preferring to stare down at her plate rather than watch the beautiful savage gorge down on his food, like the rest of his kin. But then she noticed something peculiar. Stephens was not ravaging his meat. He was, in fact, cutting at it quite delicately and with great care. He seemed to treat the meat as if it was very precious to him. This made her feel a little better and she decided to raise her head a little. "Miss Anne is a nice woman." Sen-hi commented, struggling with the fork and knife. "You're supposed to hold them like this." Stephens demonstrated, holding the fork and knife in the customary eating position. She reluctantly copied him, the copy samurai himself, and attempted to cut the meat. To her surprise, it worked rather well. There was another thing, too. She actually enjoyed doing it. Secretly, she decided that she would not allow Stephens to see her enjoying the activity and lunged the cut meat into her mouth, as if she was lunging a sword through her head. He chuckled quietly at her stubborn behavior and shook his head. "You know, you never thanked me, Sunny." Her eyes darted to him and she replied, "Thanked you? For...what?" Stephens casually stirred his grits and smiled at her. "You never thanked me for allowing you to speak in your language to me."

"I shouldn't have to...I...!" Sen-hi eyed the Captain carefully for any sign of surprise movements. She detected no malice in his voice, just a slight tinge of sarcasm. When she saw that the situation was a mere attempt at humor, she smirked in spite of herself and muttered, "Thank you, indeed, Captain. I suppose you could have done worse." Without a second between bites, Captain Stephens pointed the fork at Sen-hi. "I could have done much worse, yes. I could have left you with Lieutenant Macarthur."

"Mac...arthur." Sen-hi sneered at the sound of that man's name as she spoke it. Her eyes narrowed as she imagined her knife cutting out his heart instead of the piece of meat. "I swear upon my father's sword that I shall cut that man's head off and show it to his children before I kill them as well."

"Why the children?" Stephens threw the reply into the conversation as if what Sen-hi said didn't make a difference. Sen-hi felt the indifference of Captain Stephen's contributions and stared at him through determined and anger-filled eyes.

"Because a man like him should never know the honor or joy of having children or seeing them grow. Just as well, the seeds of such a man should not be allowed to spread and infect the rest of the Earth." Stephens shook his head and finished the last scoop of grits before he gave it to Miss Anne, who, Sen-hi was amazed to find, was constantly at the Captain's side every time he finished a plate.

"So tell me, would you think the same way of anyone who dishonored you thus? Would you cut anyone's head off and show it to their children if they..." Sen-hi stood up and slammed her hands on the table. The vibrations were enough to make even Captain Stephens shudder a little visibly, yet he seemed to keep his composure.

"If you want to know whether I wish to kill you or not, Captain

—— 34 ——

Lance Stephens, let me be blunt. The answer is an undeniable, infallible yes. Mark my words, Captain Stephens. One day, sir, you will die at my hands...at the end of my father's sword. I promise this to you." Stephens slowly got up from his table, put his hands on it and matched her gaze. Sen-hi did not waver, even at the sight of this magnificent specimen of man before her. He then lowered his voice to a pitch that she would never want to hear again.

"Pray, allow me to be blunt with you, madam. You are in my house. This house belonged to my father, my father's father and his father before him. I have worked this land myself, ground my hands to bare bone and flesh. I have survived my father and younger sisters through poverty and, finally, death. Yes, I know of death, Sunny. I know what it is like to hold a loved one in your arms and watch their last breath leave their bodies. I am all too familiar with the unpleasant task of carrying on without their unwavering guidance. You will learn to understand that you are not the only one who is suffering. You are not the only person in the world that believes that they are right and everyone else is wrong. I cannot tell you to forget Japan and accept our lifestyle just like that. But I can tell you, Sunny, that you belong here now. This is your house now just as much as it is mine, or Miss Anne's, or Miss Margaret's or any of my other servants. You will learn your place here and you will learn to mind me and do as I say. You will learn to speak proper English and you will come to me when I ask for you, but I will never ask anything improper of you, for I respect you as a warrior and Samurai. You will do all of these things, Sunny. By heaven, you will do these things or I promise you...you will regret it." With that, Captain Stephens straightened his jacket and placed his napkin on the plate.

"Now then, Miss Anne, do be a dear and take my plate to the kitchen. I have had my fill this fine evening. I will see you in the morning." Sen-hi watched in contemptuous anger as he made his way out of the dining room. He would not get the best of her, she convinced herself. This savage foreigner would never break her. Sen-hi's mind was racing with thoughts of escape and revenge as she saw Miss Anne throw what looked like a worried glance at her and glared at the Captain's departing form as Miss Anne took the plates and stepped into the kitchen.

CHAPTER FOUR
BEST LAID PLANS

Private Charles patrolled his section of Fort Francisco with ease. He had the whole route memorized, it was simple really. Little River, as it was called by the Indians and Army, meandered in front of the Fort, snaking its way along the border between the Fort and base of the Upper Messiah Mountain on the other side. The long patrol circuit that he frequented was heavily guarded by two towers which also served as the main support beams for the entrance to the fort. Upon a frontal attack, the Commander would order the massive doors closed and Charles would take his position behind one of the new Gatling Guns. On the far side of the front of the Fort, at each corner, stood watchmen on a constant vigil, searching for any signs of trouble. Lately, though, there had been few sightings of the local tribes. Having made the last leg of his patrol, Charles was about to signal the 'all clear' sign, as he always does towards the end of his post before his relief shifts with him. This time, however, it was not an all clear. Charles reeled back in pain and shock as his body was thrown backwards from an unknown object. As his back pounded against the hard wood of the platform where he walked every day, Charles looked at his chest and saw an arrow, an Indian Arrow, protruding from his chest, dripping with his blood. He managed to scream "Attack! Fortify!" as his mouth became filled with blood and then he knew no more.

The Garrison Commander, Taylor Reese was in his bunker inside the Fort when his acting Commander of the Watch ran inside with news of the attack. "Sir! Report from the watch! Attack from locals! Locations towards the North Tower are already confirmed."

"Very well, Commander. Signal the Tower Gunners to ready the artillery and do not fire until I give the word. Oh and, Commander. Ready the militia. These red bastards are not going to take us by surprise this time." The Watch Commander snapped his hand at attention, smartly turned on his boots and ran outside the tent to relay his Commander's orders.

Right Hand and Silent Eagle, one of his most trusted warriors, both watched the Fort come alive with activity after their arrow hit one of the watchers on the Towers. "It is as you predicted. The pale faces are running around like wild buffalo after one of their calves have been hit." Silent Eagle observed, patting Right Hand on the back in triumph.

"Now, the Commander will announce that the Tower weaponry will be armed and he will no doubt have that group of seasoned soldiers get ready for an oncoming assault. I think he calls them a malesha. He will not, though, be expecting us to be ready for them. Signal our men to make their attacks when the Tower Guards come into their positions. Once they are taken out, we will move in and take the Fort by force. I want the Commander alive." Silent Eagle nodded in confirmation and made hand gestures to the men around him, who quickly snaked their way closer to the Fort.

Back at the Fort, the Watch Commander, Scott Smith, relayed orders to his men, who were busy checking and re-checking the ammunition on their weapons and training them on assumptive positions of attack. Once the militia was in place in a defensive posture inside the Fort, near the center of the interior, Smith ran to the base of one of the Towers and called for the all ready. The gunners, in turn, were to use their vantage point to look for snipers or ambush raid groups and take them out. Smith nodded in satisfaction as the first Tower's Guard sounded off "Ready! Position is white!". But his relief at knowing no assailants were coming was short-lived as the last three

Towers did not sound off. Smith looked at the last three Towers and called out, "At the ready, Towers 2 through 4? Report back, do you see anything?" But they did not answer. Instead, the Gatling Guns turned towards the inside of the Fort and he assumed the worst. "Open fire on these Towers! They have infiltrated..." But he was cut off by the sound of the Gatling Guns' cacophonic, repetitive sound as the rain of bullets penetrated his body and continued their assault on the inside of the Fort.

The Indians on Towers two, three and four, pulled the massive guns towards the first Tower and destroyed them before the soldiers had a chance. The militia broke formation as they had no choice and attempted to storm the occupied Towers, but were brutally slaughtered by the merciless Gatling Guns before they could get within rifle range.

Commander Reese could hear all the gun shots and anguished screams of his men from inside his bunker and knew that something had gone horribly wrong. No soldier had entered his office to inform him of the news. He only had his three personal Guards near him and he could sense their tension. As he stood to give the order to evacuate, two of the guards collapsed to the floor dead. The one guard that was still alive held a weapon, trained on him. It was an Indian.

How did this Indian gain access to the Fort and become one of his Guards? Reese stood, trying very hard to look fearless, and looked at his would-be assailant. "I wager that as crafty as you all were to take this Fort, you must speak my language." The Indian did not speak and instead, motioned to the door, which opened to reveal another Indian with high-ranking tattoos and feathers. This, the Commander thought, must be the leader. "He will not speak to you, Commander, that pleasure is mine.", the Indian behind him said as he continued, "You will sit as I tell you how I accomplished this feat."

"I will stand", Reese stated with defiance, "...and if you don't like it, son, you can gun me down for I am an American and will not yield to the likes of you."

Right Hand's face turned to a scowl at the impudence of this pale face, but he still decided to let him live.

"Two of your Guards have always been the same, Commander, but you did not know that your third Guard, Soldier Jose Perez, was killed just earlier today. He was replaced by one of my men as we slowly and methodically made our presence into your Fort using techniques we learned from your very own military history books."

"Where did you find military books...?" The Commander asked as he saw the smile creep across the Indian's face. "You took them, didn't you? From a reservation's library. Damn you all to hell."

"No, Commander, damn you. Damn you and all the pale faces that have made it your right to take what does not belong to you. This has never been your land yet you take whatever you want without asking.

"I shall hear no more! We have never said this to be our land, Indian! We have laid claim to certain territories and have even made trade with many of your kinsmen, have given back land that was rightfully yours, so what is this really about?"

"I will show you."

Right Hand showed Reese a crudely drawn map. The map had names on it, most of which he did not recognize. One of them, however, 'Presidio', was very familiar. Right Hand noticed the Commander's facial expression and smiled. "No doubt, Commander, you noticed the name 'Presidio' on our map. We are well aware of the name of your main command headquarters' location and are also intimately aware of the schedules of each of your soldier's shifts. We even, in fact, already have men of our own inside the complex, awaiting our instructions."

Reese refused to believe these backwater redskins could have encroached that far into the Army so as to have operatives in the Presidio itself! "Tell me, young man, you say you know all these things..."

Right Hand sneered, but allowed him the courtesy to continue.

"...you know these things and have your men in place but you haven't taken everything into consideration.

You haven't told me or shown any sign of preparation for how you will answer an all-out assault by the Army or Cavalry. You do realize, do you not, that the United States will not suffer an intrusion on any of its bases for very long and, I assure you, our Government will make sure none of the people from your tribe will get one spot of land, either by force or by negotiation." Commander Reese's grit and determination was evident in the cold, granite-like stare he gave his captor. One which Right Hand attempted to match, but failed miserably. Instead, Right Hand cold-cocked the Commander across the jaw and let his head slump over into unconsciousness right there.

Silent Eagle could not contain his anxiety any longer, "Brother, all the white eye's ego aside, we cannot throw away his words so quickly. He is right. We haven't a chance against all the White Eye's forces." Right Hand holstered the Commander's weapon, smiled and unrolled a piece of the map that had previously been folded inwards, so as to appear as if it was the end of the map. "Here is our answer." Right Hand stated simply, with his defiant arm outstretched and fingers pointed to a particular area of the map. Silent Eagle's eyes grew wide with excitement when he read the words, which were in his people's language, "Tom'nee", which in White Eye speak meant, 'Gathering Tribes'. Silent Eagle looked to his leader and, as if answering his silent question, Right Hand said, "Three Months." The two men stood proudly over the first of their many prisoners, his head tilted down in defeated unconsciousness, and dreamt of many other white eye heads hung, but in death at their hands.

CHAPTER FIVE
POWER PLAYS

After not hearing any messages from his nearest Fort and Commander Reese for two weeks, Captain Stephens had become increasingly concerned. His fears were realized when a scout returned with grim news. Fort Francisco had been compromised and was crawling with hostile Indians. This could be no coincidence given the recent attacks on civilians and soldiers in the nearby mountains. After a detachment that was sent from his headquarters returned with only 2 surviving men and, on top of that, themselves severely injured and with a message from the intruders, Foreseeing the escalation of the incidents that had transpired and knowing the length of time it would take for correspondence to travel, Captain Stephens was glad he had decided weeks ago to get the General involved and had just received the letter announcing his imminent arrival.

Miss Anne and Sen-hi were in full swing getting the Captain's house in order and making it presentable and hospitable for the General's arrival. Captain Stephens had been informed by the gate watch that the General's carriage had just passed the main receiving gate and was beginning unloading. This would take some time, therefore, the Captain decided to make a formal announcement to his staff. Miss Anne and Sen-hi stood in line with the rest of the house staff and listened intently as their Master relayed their orders and his wishes.

"I do not need to tell you the importance of this visit to this house. General Thomas Nelson is an old friend and someone I have a tremendous amount of respect for. I expect his room to be clean at all times, his uniform to be pressed and duty ready at a moment's notice and his orders to be followed without question."

"While the General is here,", Stephens said, walking to each of his servants, "...you are to think of him as you do me, your Master. If he gives you an order, you are to follow it." The Captain's eyes scanned his staff's faces slowly for any sign of understanding and then stopped when he got to Sen-hi. "Do all of you understand?" Sen-hi joined her fellow staff members as they responded with a very emphatic "Yes." She knew now that the Captain was not a totally evil man, not even a tyrant like she originally thought, however, she had no intention to give her freedom up so completely. This, 'General' the Captain kept mentioning...Sen-hi wondered if maybe her freedom could be won through him somehow. She could hear the horses and booted footsteps making their way up to the front door and began formulating a plan. By the end of this meeting, both the General and the Captain would know who Sen-hi really was.

Proud Eagle shook with rage and disbelief upon hearing the news of Right Hand's treacherous attack and occupation of the white eye's base. The messenger relayed every detail of the young warrior's plan to the Elder, making sure not to leave anything out. "To think that one of our own, and my son most of all, would go this far to prove a point. He should know this kind of barbarism is not our way. I thought I had taught him better than that."

"Not all in the tribe follow and believe in the old ways anymore, wise Elder.", The young Mapiya messenger's words struck the Elder hard, making him realize that this young man too, regardless of how efficient he was at his job, may have been somewhat corrupted by Right Hand's ideas and beliefs. As the Elder listened to the rest of the messenger's tale, Spirit Bear made his presence known upon entering Proud Eagle's tent.

The Elder acknowledged his old friend and the messenger saw an opportunity for an exit.

"Brother Spirit Bear, I need your medicine now. My son, Right Hand, has lost his way and has launched a massive insurgent attack against one of the white eye bases."

"What? What do you mean?"

Elder Proud Eagle went on to detail the messenger's tale, including the details of how Right Hand already had warriors in disguise inside the base itself.

"Elder Brother, I always had my suspicions of Right Hand's beliefs, but never would I have imagined that he would have taken them this far."

"My son is disturbed apparently, but that is of no consequence. What is important, Brother Spirit Bear, is that something be done about this."

"It will not be long before the white eye comes for a blood vengeance."

Elder Proud Eagle knew exactly what the Shaman meant. There had been stories told of the white eye sending entire garrisons of troops to villages all across the country, raiding and pillaging, taking no prisoners in one village or a few women and children in another, to use as servants or translators. He was not about to allow something like that to happen to their people...his people, the Mapiya people.

"Brother Spirit Bear, I fear that drastic steps must be taken in order to undo my son's actions. These steps, though, cannot be done while I am one of a Council of Elders. I must have the ability to make the decisions necessary to protect our people." The Shaman eyed his friend warily and asked what he meant. "You must make me the Chief Elder of the Mapiya." Spirit Bear sat there for a few minutes in silence, trying very hard to understand his old friend's words.

"Wise and venerable Elder Proud Eagle, are you asking to be the one and only leader of our tribe?" His friend's stoic, determined gaze was all the answer he needed. He was indeed serious. "How do you see this as an answer to your son's departure from us?"

"As it stands, my brother and oldest friend, every decision must be ratified by our Council before it is enacted. This, in itself, is not a major problem, however, now is not the time to hear opposing viewpoints. We need unity and a single voice to guide us to the right path. If we do not do this, I fear the next buffalo hunt will be our last."

Spirit Bear cleared his throat and considered his words carefully.

"How do you propose to do this thing? The Council decides on all matters. There exists no precedent to..."

Elder Proud Eagle raised his hand and interrupted, "The Rite of Ascension."

Proud Eagle's friend never knew him to joke very much, especially during a serious conversation. The Shaman shifted uncomfortably in his squatted position and asked, "You mean for me to ask The Great Spirit for blessing and protection upon you...for...total leadership over the Council?"

"Not The Great Spirit, Shaman Spirit Bear, there is a different spirit guardian I wish the blessing from...the Raven."

Shaman Spirit Bear rustled uncomfortably in his place, in disbelief of the words he thought he just heard his old friend and leader say. He shifted his weight from one foot to the other and looked intensely into the small fire separating the two men.

"When we were younger men,", Proud Eagle explained, "I am not sure if you remember this, there was a day before the Great Hunt, during our initiation, when your Father, the Great Wise Sage and Leader, Many Eyes, asked the Raven for guidance, much as I am asking now. He stood before the fire and asked the Raven to imbue each of us with the necessary powers to vanquish the hairy buffalo beasts. As a young man, I did not fully understand what this meant or how it would help me with hunting the huge buffalo. When the ceremony ended, I could feel this indescribable power surge through my body, penetrate my muscles and I knew then nothing would stop me. When the hunt began, our group went out to the sacred hunting grounds. There, like a sea of opportunity lay our quarry. Buffalo in numbers like I had never seen before. Many of my brothers used the newfound power of the Raven poorly, they decided to rush on ahead, claim as many kills as they could, so as to make a bigger show in the Skull Dance later that night, when we arrived back home. I, however, decided to be patient. It was hard, mind you, the great power of the Raven coursed through me like liquid fire. My muscles ached to move forward, to run as fast as possible, but I willed them still. Finally, I spotted the reason for my own stillness. Ahead of me, beyond all the tumult of my brothers and their chases, there stood a lone bull. It was unlike the others. Clearly, it stood taller and broader than the rest. Upon it could be seen scars, deep gashes of battles either won, or evaded. Its face bore the story of a thousand arrows, near-misses, some even hitting their mark, only to leave a rusty surviving half arrowhead in their place. This was an old bull, a wise and powerful one. A beast filled with a medicine so virile, so potent, I knew I had to kill him, to take that medicine and make it mine. I had to be the one, just me."

Shaman Spirit Bear was already in the middle of his preparation for the Rite of Ascension during the Elder's story. He was entranced by it, knowing now that the ritual would indeed be the right thing to do. For only one such as this, his oldest friend, could have been destined to survive a fight with such a worthy adversary.

The Elder continued, "My destiny, the bull, it witnessed the chaotic carnage and stampeding around him with a kind of connected apathy, yet I could also sense he had a plan, a reason for not running off. You see, after my brothers went to kill as many buffalo as possible, they ended up scaring the rest of the lot. They managed to take many buffalo before the herd ran off, however, they may have been able to kill many more if they had been wiser and exercised caution and restraint. This bull, though, was different. Slowly, I unstrapped my initiation armor. It had been given to us by our Elder, essential, he said, to complete our ritual of the hunt. It was an encumbrance. I needed my full weight if I was to take down this monster. Slowly, I put down the bow and arrow. No cowardly attacks from a distance. Not for this one. My dagger unsheathed, I crept closer to my quarry. The bull smelled me coming, the wind was against me, but no matter. I pitted my leg against a nearby rock and lunged at the bull, arms stretched wide, my knife poised to strike. The old bison grunted angrily at my approach, stomped his feet loudly and positioned his head for a full-on ramming attack. But I was not a fellow bison about to ram him. I was a young Mapiyan, full of spirit and power. I positioned my dagger to my side and ran head on. The force of the ground shaking beneath me was unnerving. The sheer weight of the beast as it charged me would have been enough to jar any man, it took me to the boundaries of my fear. Within a fraction of time, the bull's head lunged at me and I narrowly, just by a hair on my head, escaped the goring, only to find myself flying over the beast in a tumble. It was then I realized the beast was not trying to gore me. He wanted to toss me behind him for a flanking attack. I was helpless at that point, except for one thing. I still had my dagger in my hand. As my body fell back down to the earth, I looked out the corner of my eye and spotted the creature's upper rear of his leg. With as much force as I could, I leapt up and jammed my dagger, plunged it into the nearest hard spot I could find and fell hard to the floor behind the beast, who was in the last leg of his charge. It was then that the beast reared in pain and anger. The dagger was protruding from his rear, a fresh trail of blood oozing out of the open wound."

"The Bison turned to face me again for his and charged, however, this time, his movement was slightly sluggish. I quickly took advantage of this and leapt towards the side of the beast. Part of his horn did manage to gut me in the side, but I couldn't feel the injury at that moment. I was too involved in my strategy. With all the strength I had left in me, I grabbed my dagger with both hands while my legs wrapped themselves around the beast's rear and pulled with all my might towards the front, making an enormous gash across the spine of the beast, crippling it immediately. With a mighty bellow, the beast fell to the floor and the earth thudded in protest. Now its breathing was shallow, labored. Its eyes searched me for release. I humbly gave it to him by stabbing my dagger into its brain. There lay my prize, I thought. I and I alone killed this great creature. This great ancient one that had roamed these lands unconquered was now mine to use, to show to my people as my totem for this hunt. It was that point that I knew, brother of mine, that the Raven had chosen me to be its bearer for the rest of my life; for next to the body of that animal, beside its massive body, standing atop the ground was a raven. My destiny."

Upon hearing his story, Shaman Spirit Bear knew what needed to be done. With great care, he completed the ceremony of ascension and gave his friend the power elixir to drink from.

"With this drink, you take inside of you the power of the Raven and guidance of your own totem. May you use it wisely and lead our people to their true future." In one great gulp, the Elder drank the elixir. At first, nothing happened. The Elder seemed the same as he had appeared when he first walked into the Shaman's tent. The changes only began appearing slowly, at first. Proud Eagle's right eye glistened in the darkness. An unnatural sight, to be sure. Even his pupil became an odd shape, perfectly rounded yet bigger and more black than before. The Shaman sat back in awe as he witnessed the change, then breathed a gasp of shock when he saw what happened next.

Proud Eagle's body convulsed wildly in front of the fire. The beads and totems around the tent wobbled uncontrollably, flasks and ceramic containers toppled to the floor, some breaking, others spilling their contents upon the rugs or ground beneath them. His body was going through a change, to be sure. A series of violent metamorphosis. Shaman Spirit Bear had heard of this happen before with the Rite of Ascension, but never to this degree. He sat back in a corner of the tent, which was pitching and yawing as if under attack by some ungodly wind, mouth agape at the spectacle before him. Suddenly, the fire leapt into even greater life, threatening the safety of the tent itself! From its maw, a multitude of spiritual power poured forth into the Elder's flailing body. "By the gods!" The Shaman exclaimed, shielding his eyes from the blinding light of the increased flame.

The Elder's body accepted the forms of writhing flame as they assailed him, each one granting him either a new feature on his body or accentuating and/or enhancing an existing one. It took some time, but the madness was finally over and all that was left of the craze was a smoldering fire between the two friends...and an enormous organic lump of a man where Elder Proud Eagle once stood.

"Proud Eagle? Elder? Are you...all right?" The body shifted slowly, each shoulder lifting the muscular form to a standing posture. The Shaman now saw the full effect of the Rite...and was humbled to tears. "I am better than all right, Shaman. I...am a god." With a heave of his shoulders backwards, two massive wings arced wide to both ends of the tent. They were not fake wings, not made of cloth or leather. They were wings of a bird of prey...and they were attached....to Proud Eagle. "Elder Proud..."

"Silence." The man commanded, with an almost magical voice. "That is no longer a name befitting my new station and position in the stars. My name of destiny is now and forever more, Raven Black. Inform the council I will be visiting them and taking our tribe to its new place in glory." The Shaman immediately leapt outside the tent in fear and shock and, to his surprise, found that no one outside the tent reacted as if they had any knowledge of anything had transpired. Everyone was still going about their usual routine and activities. No matter, the Shaman had a special message to deliver and none of these people could stop him...wait, he thought. 'Why am I so blindly rushing to deliver this message? He cannot be a god?" Just as he was about to come to his senses, an ethereal fog crept from the tent and invaded his mind, covering his thoughts with confusion.

'What is happening to me? It is the power of the Spirits within him! He is making me a mindless minion of the shadow! I must warn..." But that was his last free thought at the moment. At once, the fog completely enveloped him and the will-less mind and body of what once was Shaman Spirit Bear trudged towards the tent of the Council with but one thought: "Inform the Council of Raven Black's new title of Tribal Leader." It was his master's voice now that he heard inside his mind. His master's voice...and no one...and no thing else.

The Elders on the Council were often gathered together in the Communal Tent during midday. They could be found there discussing a matter of different things, from tribal activities, herd patterns and whereabouts of different local animals to other tribes that may or may not have been spotted in the area. Most pressing at this time, however, were the reports that had been coming in rather regularly from Elder Proud Eagle's son, former Elder Right Hand. Elder Sitting Moose lit his pipe and began to layout his thoughts. "It is obvious that Right Hand intends to rally the other tribes to his aide. He no doubt wishes to bring all the might of the Great Spirit's people against the white eye. We must ask here whether that is a good thing. Or whether we should be surrendering to the white eye and finally allow them to barter with us...and give them this land they want."

Elder Patient River raised his hand, "I do not think that is a wise thing, Elder. If we give our land to the white eye, he will destroy it, ravage the crops, burn all the planting fields, starve off our buffalo and take us from our birthing lands. No, I feel that we should lend aide to our former Brother and join for one final fight against these white monsters." The rest of the Elders shifted uncomfortably and murmured amongst each other. This kind of debate had been going on for almost two months now and it was getting them nowhere. They needed something to stir them into some kind of action. Then, like a bolt out of the blue sky, something sudden did come in. Shaman Spirit Bear's possessed form walked into the tent and uttered, "Brothers of the Council, behold, for Raven Black will now visit you and take his place as the new leader of the Mapiya."

The Elders all turned with rapt attention and shock at the arrival of a new figure in their tent. "Who is this, Shaman Spirit Bear? You there, who are you to intrude upon this sacred meeting, Brother?" The dark figure, imposing and full of power, was indeed a sight to behold. "Look, brothers! His feet do not touch the ground! He is enchanted with dark powers! Do not..." With a crack of lightning from his fingertips, the dark figure pointed his arms at the protesting Elder, whose body jolted at the attack, then crumpled upon the floor, a smoking, dead heap. "Who...are you?"

"Do you not recognize me, my brothers?" The stranger slowly uncovered his face, lowering the cloak that had been covering his head and the Council visibly gasped. "The Elder you knew is gone. Elder Proud Eagle is no longer among you. He has been chosen as the vessel of a new power for the Mapiya...for all men of the spirit. This power now asks...commands that you obey me. For I am now the sole voice of this once former Council."

The Council members blanched at the sight before them and they could also feel a very palpable, powerful presence before them. Elder Sitting Bear was familiar with this kind of power and, being the oldest voice on the council, decided he needed to act now before it was too late. "Elder Proud Eagle, I do not know what you have done to change this much, but this farce ends now. This Council will not be swayed by your threats, I say now that..."

With the swiftness of a bird of prey, Raven Black outstretched his fingers and another crack of lightning erupted from his fingertips and struck Elder Sitting Bear with astonishing force. The blow made the Elder's body jerk about wildly and the other Elders backed away in terror. Now, where the Elder was, a black clump of ash lay. Raven Black looked around the room at where the other Council Members were cowering in fear and smirked in confidence, "Now that you see a hint of my new powers, do any of you have any other doubts?" Not a word came from the members and with that, Raven Black had become the solitary new leader of the Mapiya Tribe.

Across the vast terrain, inside the occupied Fort Francisco, Elder Right Hand could feel a massive change in the wind. His friend, Silent Eagle, noticed his grave expression and asked, "What is amiss, brother?"

"I felt a sudden change in the winds, something odd is happening but I am unsure what to make of it."

"Do not be troubled, brother Right Hand. The other tribal leaders have already sent scouts here in approval of your call of unity and we should be seeing the warriors upon our doorsteps any day now."

"Good, when they arrive, we march on the Garrison Commander's Base and take back this land from the white eye."

CHAPTER SIX

VINDICATIONS AND REVELATIONS

General Thomas Nelson was not known as the superstitious type. His experience with the supernatural was limited to sparse occurrences of strange comets flying across the vast night sky during many nights out in the open prairie. Nelson was known by many in his regiment as a 'hard bear' of a man. He was fast on the draw, faster on his feet and fastest to wit. There wasn't, it was said, a man alive that could out-think, out-gun or out-run General Thomas Nelson. There was, in fact, a rumor that he earned the field commission of General from a foot race that he won against a certain flat-footed, snooty Fort Commander by the name of Custer. By and large, the news of one of his Forts being invaded and occupied for nearly a month rested none-too-easy on the General's mind. This visit to his Captain's residence and main base of operations near the Presidio was anything but pleasant, but it had to be done.

Captain Stephens' head servant, Miss Anne, opened the door with all the poise and grace she could muster. There, standing on the threshold, was a marvel of a man. General Thomas Nelson was welcomed into the home with all the pomp and pleasantry she could think of. He smiled courteously and gave the former slave his hat and gloves. "Captain Stephens," The General saluted, "I think it best to skip the formalities for now. Let's get to business."

The Captain smartly returned the salute, the two sat opposite each other in the main drawing room and Stephens filled the General in as best as he could.

"Far as we know sir, as per our last communication, Fort Francisco is still occupied with the hostile force that invaded it. The Fort Commander is still alive and in moderately stable health. Our sources that have been secretly spying on the Fort report that the main Indian, a Silent Eagle, as he is called, means to keep the Fort occupied as long as possible in the hopes that we give up the position. They then maintain to do similar attacks to other Forts, until they at last reach here. Or such is their plan. I intend to mount a full-scale assault on the Fort immediately upon your approval and get back what's rightfully ours."

"A well-thought-out plan, to be sure, Captain, however your information is severely lacking in clarity."

"Sir?"

"Firstly, the leader of the Indians is not Silent Eagle. He is the second-in-command, at best. The actual leader is named Right Hand. He is the son of a local Mapiya Elder, Proud Eagle. Apparently, this Elder's son broke rank and invaded our Fort for the sole purpose of gaining confidence and leverage with the other tribes. Within this month, Captain, this young Indian has amassed several tribes already within the Fort and is, as we speak, is positioning his men for a full-on assault on this base....within this week perhaps."

Captain Stephens balked at this piece of news. "Sir, how can this be? How did you come to this information?"

"I have my own scouts, Captain. I must, apparently, give them to you since it is obvious your scouts are incompetent and slow."

"General, I am at a loss."

"Indeed you are if you go along with your plan. It's what he wants and expects. I have come here, Captain, because you will need my own personal garrison of men to complement your own if you are to stop this madman."

"Sir, I assure you, I do not need two garrisons of men to stop one crazed Indian and a few ragtag groups of rebel tribes from..."

"I beg to differ, Captain Stephens."

The two men turned in surprise to another voice that lent its opinion to the conversation. The General smirked in amusement, while the Captain's face grew beet red in anger as they looked upon Sen-hi.

"Forgive me for intruding, Captain, however, I did want to show you how much progress I have made in my English. I feel it is going rather well, don't you think?"

"Um..yes, well, General, you'll forgive my servant's..."

"I am not your servant, Captain. I am your Guest. That much I assure you. General Nelson, if you will permit me to speak, I will tell you why I feel that even your plan, while a good one at its basic root, needs more substance if it is to succeed.."

"You impudent little..." The Captain raised his hand to strike Sen-hi, however, she was quicker. Without him realizing, Sen-hi brought out the hidden sheathed sword she had tucked away in the folds of her dress and blocked the Captain's outstretched arm with skill. The General, while taken aback by her boldness, was very impressed by her ability.

"I thought I took that away from you." Captain Stephens seethed, staring with contempt at the sheathed weapon.

"I took it back, Captain. I told you I would not suffer your behavior towards me much longer. Now, you will permit me my words with your General, sir..."

"I will do no such thing! What does a woman, and a foreigner, to boot, know about..."

"Enough, Captain. I already know of this woman and the truth of her presence here among us via your correspondence to me some months ago. I feel it would be prudent to hear her out. Besides...it's not every day your best Captain gets a lesson in discipline from a woman."

"General, I assure you that I..."

"Enough, Captain. You had better have a good explanation why you took it upon yourself to not only treat this woman the way you have, but also make her a house slave."

The Captain sighed and decided that, finally, he had better come clean. It appeared that his career would depend on it. "General... and Miss Sakeda," Sen-hi, upon hearing her name said with such politeness for the first time since setting foot on American soil, sunk to the sofa in tears.

"Thank you. Captain, thank you for using a title with...with my name." The Captain shrugged, then smiled slightly and continued,

"I had every intention of giving Sen-hi all the formalities even though my actions have been to the contrary. However, I also am a soldier and a Captain and I am an American...all those things come first, come before my duties as a diplomatic escort. Do they not, General?"

"Go on."

"I read the reports of her actions and behavior upon entering our country, I saw for myself her rash and, yes, even barbaric behavior towards my countrymen at the docks and felt she had no knowledge of diplomacy, not even of common courtesy. I felt it necessary to teach this young lady some manners...my way. My Father, you know, was a very stern man. Whenever he taught me a lesson, he made damn sure I kept the lesson for the rest of my days. He went the extra mile to teach me right from wrong, how to treat people and, most of all, how to be treated."

The Captain then turned his attention to Sen-hi and said, "As to how I bested you, Sen-hi, I feel I should clarify certain things. When I was stationed in Japan, I learned the ways of the sword from watching someone perform your techniques, this much you already know."

"Captain, forgive me for interrupting, but I still do not understand how you could learn such a sacred technique by just observing it." Sen-hi stated.

Instead of giving her a look of anger, though, the Captain merely nodded in acceptance and went on to explain,

"It's true, the Samurai are severely stubborn in their secrets. The answer is that I didn't really beat you. My sword did." Captain Stephens walked over to the table in between the sofas and pushed in a small panel. The table opened up and two swords were revealed, the very same ones Sen-hi and the Captain sparred with about a month ago.

The Captain took them out and handed them to the General and Sen-hi. Sen-hi immediately felt the heaviness of the sword, just like before. For the first time, though, Sen-hi noted something very different about the sword she was holding. On the hilt, there was a hidden compartment. Upon closer inspection, she discovered there was, "A strength dampening device of my own construction", Stephens seemed to answer her thoughts,

"Powered by miniature gears, which are, in turn, empowered by runes, which are only visible in moonlight." The General inspected his sword and saw a similar compartment. Before the Captain could explain, the General said, "And this one, I wager, has a strength and... well, perhaps maybe speed enhancer?" He figured, swinging the sword at a quicker-than-normal speed.

"Very well deduced, sir. It's actually just a magnetizing agent, again, powered by runes. This makes any swords you fight against a natural repellant. Anyone fighting with that sword already has an advantage. Even the most seasoned fighter would find it difficult to deflect such a weapon."

"Brilliant work, Captain. But something puzzles me. How did you manage to make such weapons and why is this the first I've heard of it?"

Captain Stephens was a tad bit confused as to why the General wasn't more surprised at these weapons, but he continued, "Frankly, sir, they are still in the working phase. I do not have enough resources to make more. I found the runes inscribed inside a mountain which..."

"Which the Mapiya people must frequent..did I guess right, Captain Stephens?" Sen-hi added. The Captain nodded with a visibly impressed look.

"Excellent, Sen-hi, yes. It's one of the main reasons I've been sending men to that mountain and excavating from there on a regular basis. We've been discovering runes the deeper we go inside the mountain. It can only mean that, perhaps, Vikings, or someone of that culture, once inhabited this area."

"This is extraordinary. To think that we have actual real magical weapons and the ability to make them. Do you realize what this means?" The General posed.

"Although it is true that the runes have power...it is also true that their power is limited. I have tried inscribing these very same runes on other weapons, however, the runes do not imbue those other ones with the same power. It appears the runes can only be used on one weapon at a time."

"If you wish to imbue multiple weapons..." Sen-hi surmised, "You would have to either destroy the weapon once imbued..or find other new runes to use."

"Precisely."

"And that explains why owning the land that mountain resides on is of such vital importance and..." Sen-hi said.

"And why the Mapiya must be moved out of the nearby valley.", General Nelson added. "They must never know of the powers within that place. If they did...heaven help us."

"How do you know they don't already know of the power there?", Sen hi asked.

"Explain, Sen-hi." The General urged.

"It is reasonable to conclude that these 'Indians', as you call them, already know of the power residing within the mountain. It may be the reason, in fact, why they decided to live so close to it. You've said yourself your men were killed while already inside the mining tunnels you caved out and with Indian weapons. That would mean to me that the Indians already knew of the significance of the mountain or, if not before...they surely know of it now. I would not be surprised if, in this next battle, your men encounter some similar magic. I would advise severe caution before you undertake this campaign, General. Make sure your men are armed well before going into battle."

The General smiled and responded, "Do not worry, young Samurai. I may have just learned of this magical weapon today, however, my scientists and inventors had already developed some pretty damn impressive machinery and weapons well before this whole mess got started. In fact, Captain, it's one of the reasons you didn't hear from me sooner. Only a select few know of what I am referring to, very secret. If you follow me outside, I'll show you what I mean." The Captain and Sen-hi walked outside the house, following the General and stood breathless at the porch. Just outside the Captain's mansion and dotting the main interior of the receiving courtyard were a rather impressive amount of strange-looking machines, huge metal monsters, with tracks and gears for wheels and enormous barrels jutting out the top portion of the majority of them. Others looked even stranger still, Steam-powered miniature locomotives, it seemed, with more barrels and some type of rotating gun positioned on each side of the locomotive machine's main chassis. The other machines were impossible to describe, for neither the Captain nor Sen-hi had ever seen anything like them before.

The General gave them enough pause to consider the massive army in front of them and explained, "Captain Stephens, Sen-hi, what you see before you is the product of decades of blood, sweat and tears; the fruits of massive labor and culmination of some of our best scientific minds. During the war, we were caught by surprise by the Confederacy's use of steam-powered technology and weaponry. Their underwater fleet of assassin machines were a decisive call to action. We have amassed a great cache of military technology and ingenuity, all from some recent discoveries that, if they had been left undiscovered, would have left us bereft of a real future for our country, not to mention mankind as a whole. Now, with these Steam War Machines, we will be nigh-invincible! This, my friends, is America's future secured!"

Sen-hi was put off by the General's grandiose method of speech, but marveled at the sight before her. She wondered to herself if her people had these machines, would there have been as many casualties during the Meiji Restoration. With this and the few rune-powered weapons on their side, Sen-hi did not think the Mapiya people stood a chance. For the first time since arriving here, she began to feel pity for them.

Half a state away, a month had passed since the Mapiya had their new leader in Raven Black. With most of the neighboring tribes already absorbed in the Mapiyan territories and the Sacred Mountain guarded heavily, the Mapiyan Leader had one more obstacle to remove: the encroaching Fort Haven, one of the main bases near the Mountain, the one commanded by a certain Captain Stephens, according to the white eye prisoner.

Raven Black's visions had increased in frequency and intensity.

Through them, the spirits of shadow would show him some of the mighty metal monstrosities he would encounter in this battle to come. Instead of being worried, though, the Mapiyan Chief smiled. Emerging from his tent, Black stepped into a village filled with Indians who were once separated by tribal in-fighting but now were united and armed with stronger bows and arrows, glowing and pulsating with dark energy, horses with skin-colored covers on their sides to hide their skins that were actually covered in checkered purple and black patterns of infectious dark power. There was also one particular item, a massive monstrosity completely covered in a huge tarp, that the Chief was saving for a special occasion. Surrounded by the awesome enormity of his new future, a vision overtook Black's senses.

A black sea stood before Raven Black. Looking out into the vast openness before him, the Mapiya leader searched for a mark, a sign of land anywhere in the distance. There was none to be seen. Instead, there was a calming wave over the water, lapping to the shore on which Black stood. In one hand, he held a sword of unknown origin. On the other hand, he held the tribal standard of his people, which had a mountain in the foreground with a brilliant sun rising behind it. On top of the mountain, an eagle was perched, a symbol of their connection with the free spirit of the land itself. On closer inspection of the sword on his other hand, Black noticed it was the exact same sword that had pierced through his son's body in the vision he had many moons ago. This time, he was holding it. This time, he felt control and power in its grasp. A call came out over the waters ahead of him. It sounded like a call to war. Black raised his hands, ready to do battle with whatever or whoever were to come his way.

Emerging from the inky black sea came a cloaked figure, with wings as black as ash, not unlike his own wings. Black stepped back, startled at what approached. "What...who is this come before me?" He demanded, his eyes glowing with burning rage. The figure stood motionless, merely an arm's reach from Black. From within the billowing hood, a deep, scathing, rasping voice responded, almost in a mocking tone, "Who is this come before me?"

Raven Black scoffed at the figure's impudence. "How dare you? Do you not know this is my vision, spirit? Speak, I command it!"

"Be silent, mortal man.", the figure said. In an instant, Black's ability for speech was taken from him. His arms and legs became bound by an unseen, but terrifyingly powerful force. His eyes searched wildly in terror, looking for a way out, but there was none. There was only the figure.

"Raven Black, you are an ungrateful human to speak to me thus. I, who gave you the power you now possess, I who gave you the control over the tribes that you now have. You, mortal, should be on thy knees thanking me for what I have done for thee."

Suddenly, Black found himself on his knees, against his will. A tear of fright escaped his face and, in that second of time, or at least it felt like that, he felt the weight of his age upon him.

"In the blink of an eye...in the very space and breadth of that tear on thy face, Raven Black, we can take back all that we have given thee."

Raven Black found his voice again and pleaded, "No, please, forgive me my impertinence, great one! I am merely a man and did not know I was speaking to The Great Spirit!" Then, he felt the surge of power within him again. This time, however, he kept the scant trace of humility for the figure...or...was it, rather, reverent fear?

"We are not The Great Spirit. The Great Spirit did not deem you worthy of such power, leader of the Mapiya. He did not feel you were pure of heart to obtain such a gift."

"Then...how?" Black wondered.

"Did you not ask assistance of the Raven in the Rite of Ascension?"

Black nodded and the dark figure continued, "The Great Spirit is not the only one who can bestow gifts, oh meager one. It is within all of the gods' will and might to bestow such things to man. We have done so in the past many times and have decided to intervene once again."

"Why? Why choose me, oh mighty one?"

The figure's wings contracted slightly, a chill in the air bit at the very heart of the Mapiyan Leader. "We 'chose' you because you possess the ambition we crave. Your body was the right make for the transformation you are going through and, most of all, because you are the only one who can stop the Champion of The Great Spirit."

"Champion?"

"Yes. The sword in your right hand. Look upon it." Raven Black slowly brought the sword to his line of sight and looked at it. It was a truly beautiful weapon. The design was slightly familiar. The sword was made out of some kind of hardened wood and, around the blade itself was covered in sharp pieces, black-as-ash, acting like a kind of 'teeth' for the sword. The hilt was made out of a rock-like substance, harder than most spears and arrowheads. The sheath was fashioned, it seemed, out of a buffalo skin, with tribal marking on it. "I have never seen its like."

"No one in America has. It is a weapon once used by a people that live south of Mexico. They are called the Aztecs. The sword's blade itself is made out of hardened redwood, smoothed from the resin of the strongest oak. The pieces of black rock you see that are stuck into the wood are actually an ancient metal called "Obsidian". It is made from volcanic rock and is the sharpest, strongest metal on Earth. With this weapon, you will be invincible against the light gods' champion."

"It looks formidable, but couldn't the sword be defeated by simply exposing the wooden weak points?"

The figure quickly took out a sword and sliced at Black. Instinctively, the leader lifted the obsidian sword to block the attack and, surprisingly to him, the sword held back the swing. The wooden part of the blade deflected the attack and, what's more, it didn't even show a dent. The sword was indeed powerful!

Raven Black marveled at the weapon in his hands and knew that, with a weapon like this and the army he forged at his side, he would be unstoppable.

"When you wake from this vision, you will find yourself properly equipped."

"Just show me that Champion."

"When the time is right, Raven Black, she will come to you." In a sudden torrent of black smoke, Raven Black awoke from his vision.

He found himself sitting in his war tent, surrounded by the skulls of dead enemies he had already killed. In front of him, glowing with power, was the very same sword he saw in his vision. Beside it was a crate his tribal scouts extracted from the mountain cave the white eye had been using. Sliding the crate open, a glowing dark purple light could be seen emanating from within. The Mapiyan Leader inserted his hand into the crate and extracted a large, pulsing, glowing purplish-black stone from within. Turning it over in his hands, he instantly recognized it as the same metal from which his new sword had been made. His newfound powers also enabled him to feel and recognize the qualities and properties of the metal. *'With these ancient stones,',* a grating, dark voice uttered in his mind, *'you will create a new power for your tribe. With it...'*

"No force on Earth will be able to stop us." Raven Black finished the voice's inner thought, reveling in the grand scheme being concocted in his dark mind.

Weeks had passed since Captain Stephens' forces had amassed in several encampments within the base of the mountain, half a mile from the entrance of the compromised Fort Francisco, which now resembled more an advanced tribal fort than an army fort he had ever known.

Companies of men marched in formation throughout each tented regiment. Patrols of seasoned soldiers stood watch in the hastily-built, but sturdy, watch towers adorning the entrances of each of the regiments. In the center of the entire Brigade was the Captain's tent. Inside, Captain Stephens and General Nelson stood in front of a mapped layout of the area, the fort included. The map was dotted with different colored flags and markings, each indicating either a checkpoint for troops, invasion entry points for different companies or extraction points for captured soldiers within the fort itself. Sen-hi was sitting in the corner, carefully cleaning her legendary sword, while the Captain and General briefed each Company's Commanding Officer within the tent. The Officers were all seasoned soldiers, each with grim experience in the recent Civil War.

"Once, some of you fought either with the Confederacy or Union Army in our country's gravest war to date. Once you fought to keep your freedoms, whatever they may be. Look to the man on your side, men." The Officers turned and looked.

"The man at your side may have once been an enemy soldier, perhaps, however, you are all brothers in arms now. Put aside any old grudges you may have carried, gentlemen. We face a new threat now. These Indians have captured one of our most important bases, a Fort commanded by one hell of a Commander. We want him back alive, be very clear about that. We won't get out of this without losing some of our own, though. Mark me. Those red bastards may take hundreds of us down with their damned primitive weapons, however, we won't let them get away with it. You promise me, men. You promise me that for every single American life they take, you take 10 of them with you!"

The Officers all cried in a rallied frenzy upon hearing their General's words. With a snappy salute, the General dismissed them and turned his attention towards the Captain.

"Inspiring, sir. Truly."

"Yes, well, it's just words, Captain Stephens. It won't mean a damned thing if we don't take back that Fort. Now, on to the matter of your mission."

"Yes, sir. The Company I will be commanding will be infiltrating the auxiliary entrance, around the back, near this forested enclosure here.." Stephens pointed at a thatch-patterned area on the map, just behind the Fort. The General nodded and Stephens continued, "We'll split into teams of 5 and infiltrate key positions on each tower, as well as the internal entrenched positions they will have crafted to defend with. Three teams will be the choke point, barraging the trenched positions, bringing us cover fire, while the key team, made up of 10 of my most seasoned officers and myself, will infiltrate the main quarters and free the Fort Commander, at that point capturing the Fort and turning it to friendly side."

Sen-hi listened intently to the plan, a well-concocted one, she had to admit. The General, however, looked slightly concerned.

"Captain, while your key team is taking position to take the main quarters, who will be supporting the barrage team as they make their escape?" Captain Stephens was not expecting the question and searched the map for a free group. There was none to be found. "Sir, I..."

"Fret not, Captain, such is the reality of battle. It's a good attack plan. We initiate the initial attack formation and infiltrate the Fort openly from our current position, open flanks on the friendly side of fire, to give our boys in the Howitzers some maneuvering room."

The Captain nodded as the General continued, "You with your teams will invade with stealth during the onslaught and take back the Fort. Well done. Now, we require an Assassin." Sen-hi raised her head and met with the General's eyes.

"Oh yes, my dear. I believe in this, you will be most serviceable to us." She slowed her cleaning and listened as the General summed, "As Captain Stephens and his extraction team mount their assault, I have a very special mission for you. One that will employ your very unique set of skills." As the General outlined his plan, Sen-hi finished cleaning her sword and sheathed it with confidence. Finally, she reveled, she would see battle.

CHAPTER SEVEN

THE BATTLE AT
LITTLE RIVER

ATTACK! The Chevaux-de-Frise defenses quickly opened up to reveal a mass of armed men and Flying Battery reinforcements charging towards the river clearing separating the Fort from the base of the mountain. Already, the soldiers could hear the twang and release of the Indians' bows and arrows. The arrows rained down like a ferocious torrent, hitting as many men as they missed. Onward, the companies of men charged, not once breaking the ranks.

"Keep charging until we hit the shoreline of the river! We need to build that bridge to get these batteries set up!", one of the Lieutenants yelled, brandishing his saber forward. The horses burdened with the huge battery canons and artillery stores snorted and galloped in a hurried pace. Their drivers snapped the reins with a determined gait. Every arrow dodged added motivation to their charge.

Across the river, some distance from Fort Francisco's entrance, three rows of Mapiyan Bowmen crouched behind their makeshift defenses. Row after row, the men stood to unleash their volley of arrows at the oncoming horde. Behind them, Howling Wolf sat mounted on his loyal steed. The arrows blanketed the skies with each command he gave. So many soldiers fell that Howling Wolf thought they may win this battle without one soldier setting foot across the river. In the distance, behind the charging enemy and silhouetted by the sun, were strange looking hills and...tents, perhaps? Upon continued inspection, he noticed them acting very unlike hills and tents. They were moving.

Inside the former Fort Commander's tent, Right Hand and Commander Reese could hear faint sounds of gunfire and tribal commands coming from outside the Fort. The Commander glanced over at his captor through bruised eyes and noticed the tensed muscles and nervous apprehension of the unavoidable invasion to come.

"Look, if you give yourself up now, I promise I will tell my Commanding Officer you treated me...fairly." Right Hand did not turn to regard his prisoner, instead, he relayed orders to one of his adjutants, who quickly left the quarters to carry them out.

"Commander, I've no doubt your friends will infiltrate our formidable forces and maybe even enter the internal compound, however..." Right Hand slowly made his way to a crate near the quarter's window and creaked it open. As he did, Commander Reese could spy a glint of bright purplish light coming from within. The Commander looked on as the light from an object that had been inside the crate enveloped the Indian, transforming his native outfit into an unrecognizable leathery, but very sturdy-looking, armor set. In the Indian's hands, a short weapon of some sort emerged, glowing. It looked like a crude crossbow, yet the arrows were all glowing of the same purplish-black pigment. Right Hand slowly made his way to the Fort Commander and readied his weapon for battle as he concluded, "...however, they will be very sorry they ever crossed our people. The warriors of the shadow!"

Howling Wolf's defensive strategy was coming apart at the seams right in front of him. The new weapons that emerged in the battlefield were acting as impenetrable shields for each and every arrow they loosed. To make matters worse, the metal behemoths were trampling all in their path. It was just a matter of time before they crossed the river. Just when the Indian Commander was about to signal retreat, streaks of glowing dark light flew across the air, they almost grazed his sides in fact. Howling Wolf's nearest warriors flinched in surprise when they saw the streaks and looked on as the light trails made their impact through several soldiers at once and deep into the huge metal monsters that had just earlier seemed impregnable!

"Brother Howling Wolf, what was that?" One of the Mapiyan warriors inquired. Howling Wolf was still in shock, looking on as the white eye soldiers hastily regrouped, trying to find cover from the barrage of dark purple lights still making their screaming volley across the field of battle. He looked around, when his eyes met someone he was familiar with. It was his tribal brother and commander, Right Hand. He was glowing from head to foot in a strange suit of armor. "Come, my brother.", Right Hand stated in an almost unearthly tone as he walked towards Howling Wolf. "Share in the future of our people...and in the future of all humanity." Before Howling Wolf could protest, Right Hand slapped a piece of stone onto his friend's hand. Howling Wolf looked on in horror as his hand, then his arm, then his entire body became completely covered in dark purple patches of color. Before long, he was wearing a similar suit of armor and everything became clear.

"Thank you, my brother. I see now. Should we bring in our other brothers with us?"

Right Hand shook his head and led his friend back towards the Command Headquarters. "We have plenty of fodder to throw at the enemy. They will never defeat this new power and enough of the non-initiated will fall before we win this day. Besides, there is a more important task ahead of us."

"More important than defeating and destroying the white eye, Shadow Brother?"

"Yes, my Nagi. My new Brother. Our new Shadow Father, Our Nagano, Raven Black, has given us a new mission."

"Tell me so that I may execute it perfectly."

Right Hand pointed at the headquarters bunker and smiled as a dark pall came over his face. "In there, we will find our destiny. We must meet it...and destroy it."

"For the all-living, all honor and glory." Howling Wolf uttered. The two Shadowmen Warriors walked, like men possessed, towards the headquarters bunker, putting away their handmade crossbow weapons and made ready their brand new blackened sabers, gifted by the dark powers. Not one of the other Mapiyan warriors, men who were not yet turned, noticed the difference in their brothers.

They didn't notice their fellow Mapiyan brethren being turned to Shadowmen one by one by others already imbued, nor did they notice how Right Hand and Howling Wolf no longer cast any shadows on the ground...nor did they notice...their own transformation.

The majority of the other groups had infiltrated the main part of the river crossing. It was only a matter of time until they made the full crossing and took the entrance of the Fort itself. Sen-hi, however, was more concerned with the task given her. She looked at the small group of men assigned under her and gave each of them specific jobs. Most of them took the assignments with some animosity for her gender giving THEM an order, but they nodded their confirmation anyway. Her second-in-command, Captain Jonathan Knight, listened carefully as she outlined her plan of attack. Patiently, they waited for Captain Stephen's force to sound the call of incursion, the signal that they finally took the main river line directly in front of the Fort. Just like clockwork, the bugle horn trumpeted wildly in the distance; the call was given.

Sen-hi's band of men fanned out like ghosts, crouched low, making their footfalls silent and their weapons muffled. Straight ahead was the one weak point of the Fort: a small gaping hole in its structure, used as an old sewer line. The Mapiyans didn't recognize it for what it was and did not recognize that it was not in use. Her men stealthily made their way inside the Fort and were met with some resistance from some Mapiyan Guards patrolling nearby. The guards called out the invasion to their brothers and the number of Mapiyans almost doubled. Sen-hi predicted this would happen, though. Immediately, half of her force emerged from hiding in some of the taller trees just beyond the hole they had entered and unleashed a deadly volley of arrows and bullets at the oncoming Mapiyans. Sen-hi rushed on, not yet un-sheathing her sword, kicking or punching her way through. It wasn't until she got within sprinting distance of the headquarters that she eventually stopped. In front of her was a sizable group of Mapiyans, however, she puzzled about their appearance. These warriors were wearing some kind of leathery armor, it covered them much like any standard issue jacket would cover an infantryman, however, it had a sturdiness and heartiness to it. The warriors seemed to be equipped with some form of sabers or swords, very odd weaponry for Indians, she thought. Hanging on a sling of sorts was another odd weapon that looked very much like a crossbow. Their skin was the strangest still. Sen-hi had to get closer to be sure, but it appeared as if they were covered in patches of some kind of dark purple tattoo. Their faces bore the same marking, mostly around the eyes, like a tanuki bear would wear.

It wasn't until she engaged them in combat, that she truly realized what she was dealing with. In one sweeping motion, one of the dark warriors un-sheathed their saber and cut off the legs of five of Sen-hi's group. They fell to the floor, flailing, screaming in agony, but not for long, for the dark Mapiyans silenced them forever with quick, precise cuts across their necks. Just when one of them, who Sen-hi assumed was the lead of this group, raised his saber to strike down yet another man, his blade twanged in protest against an unexpected object: Her sheath.

Sen-hi glared at her foe and smirked, "I am aware that you may not understand my words, painted one, however, I trust you will understand my OTHER language." Without giving her enemy a chance to respond, Sen-hi used her sheath as a weapon and performed a very specific move: "Sakeda Ryu, Souin no Sen!" In a blinding motion, the sheath acted very like the butt end of a broom and literally swept the Mapiyans in front of her off the ground, pounding violently back to the very dirt they were once upon. Without a second's pause, Sen-hi used her sheath yet again and cracked their legs all at once. Her remaining men followed her as they left the enemy to their broken limbs and were at the Command Quarter's door.

Sen-hi kicked down the door with her foot and dove head first into the room, expecting a barrage of bullets to fly her way. They did not. Instead, Sen-hi landed in a flip on the other side of the room that had all its furniture cleared. On the other end of the room were two men. Both had the same dark purple patches on their skin, sabers and crossbows.

One, Sen-hi concluded, must be Right Hand, the leader of the rebel Indians. As she scanned the two men in front of her, her group joined her in the room. Almost immediately, the other man looked at his cohort and nodded. The cohort turned around and, as he did, a strange, elliptical shape manifested behind them. The shape was floating in mid-air and some kind of field with small tribal huts could be seen inside of the shape. The cohort grabbed the Fort's Commander, turned to smile at Sen-hi and her men and casually walked through the floating opening, with Commander Reese's unconscious head bobbing as he was being dragged behind the Indian.

Before Sen-hi could follow, the leader put himself between her and the opening.

"No, my dear. You will find it impossible to follow my brother in there. You will need to defeat us both before you do that." Captain Knight, Sen-hi's second-in-command, was already in the room and was dumbfounded at all of this witchcraft he just witnessed. Regardless, he could count and he only saw one Indian in the room. "You need to go back to our schools, Indian. There's only one of you and a whole lot of us!" Almost as if on cue, a tall, dark form of a man stepped through the opening in the room behind the leader. Just as he entered, the opening closed behind him. The man lifted his head and Captain Knight gasped in shock. "Elder...Proud Eagle?" I almost didn't recognize you? You look different. And...what..how in the hell did you get here?!"

A devilish, booming laugh came from the man, who sat in the now vacant seat, which had been used by the Fort's Commander.

"I would give you the details, Captain, but, I fear there is far too much trouble you're to be in now and it will be keeping you...busy. Son, you will show these men the truth of our new power, won't you?"

"Yes, Father. I will make you proud."

Sen-hi tensed her hold on her sheath as the leader, the son of this 'Elder Proud Eagle', unsheathed his saber and stood apart from her and the group.

"No, son, we don't have time for a long, drawn-out fight. Dispatch her quickly."

Right Hand placed his sheathed saber on the table where his Father was and took out his rifle.

Sen-hi saw no other recourse. She unsheathed her sword, the legendary Sakeda Blade, looking without fear at the specter of death that her foe and his leader represented.

Right Hand made a gesture towards her sword, "A beautiful weapon you have there, my dear. A pretty thing like you should be using that sword to chop vegetables, not enemies."

Sen-hi closed her eyes in silent meditation and responded, with a voice grave as death, "No. You are wrong. A sword is a weapon of death. The art of swordsmanship is only to learn how to kill. That is the only truth of a sword."

Captain Knight and the rest of Sen-hi's group looked on as, in the blink of an eye, the Indian fired his weapon and a flash of light could be seen between the Indian and Sen-hi. A tense few seconds passed with nothing happening between the two opponents. The Captain, however, noticed a look of concern come over Proud Eagle, sitting in the desk next to the Indian leader. Right Hand looked on in shock as his rifle split in two right before him.

Proud Eagle took the saber, unsheathed it and gave it to the Indian leader. Sen-hi immediately sheathed her sword and stood at the ready.

"Sen-hi, be careful, I don't know what those patches on their skin mean, but it can't be good!"

Sen-hi nodded a confirmation at Captain Knight, not once wavering in her stance. She had been in this predicament before and knew to never underestimate her opponent. Right Hand positioned himself in a rather defensive stance. Not one typically used by Samurai, of course, but one that Sen-hi recognized all the same. With his saber above his head, he made it clear he preferred a defensive strategy. He wanted to learn about her style of fighting first, apparently. Fine by her.

"Sakeda Ryu, Ichiro No Sen." In a blinding motion, Sen-hi un-clipped her sheathed sword and thrust it forward, in the direct line of her opponent's defensive space. Right Hand immediately brought his saber down to parry, however, he was surprised to discover no object there to parry against. In the same blinding second of her thrust, Sen-hi had, without him seeing, turned her weapon vertically and brought it to the side, thereby allowing his saber to pass right through the air between them, leaving his sides completely vulnerable. "Sakeda Ryu, Kaze No Shisatsu."

Before Right Hand could recuperate and literally within a half of a second, Sen-hi stabbed his side with the tip of the hilt of her sword and hit him so hard that Right Hand was thrown back against the wall with a thud. Sen-hi thought it odd, though, that there appeared no welt or bruise where her hilt hit.

Right Hand was absolutely baffled by what he had just witnessed. He immediately checked himself for injuries and winced when his hand found the internal bruise left by her still-sheathed weapon.

"I have just given you two chances at surrender. Be aware that I have, as of yet, to brandish my weapon, yet I have already done damage to you, with just the tip of my sword's hilt. Bring back the Commander at once or my next attack will not be as forgiving." "You are acting rather bold for such a lucky strike, my new victim."

"Now, now, son. Don't kill her, we could use someone like her on our side."

Right Hand looked over at his Father, who took out a small, sharp piece of dark purple stone and placed it one the desk.

"Understood, Father. She will be one of us, I swear it."

Sen-hi stood her ground, never once looking away from her opponent. She then puzzled as she saw the patch-filled Indian close his eyes and mutter something incoherent. Soon, though, his body began to glow a very faint light purple hue. In a blinding motion, Right Hand swooped upon Sen-hi in an ungodly slicing arc with his saber. It took all of Sen-hi's defensive skills just to stop him from breaking through.

"Penetrate her defenses, son!" The man at the desk shouted, banging his fist in protest. Just as quickly as he was upon her, Right Hand brought forth his hand in between them, letting forth a wave of force, shoving Sen-hi against the wall with a frightening thud. Sen-hi tried to get herself up and shake off the blow, however, as she lifted her head to re-orient herself, her opponent was already upon her and, this time, he was wielding a different weapon. It was a small, sharp stone, the very same one from the desk.

Her men immediately came to her aid, raising their guns to

dispatch him. It was for nothing, as with a simple gesture of his arm, Right Hand sent the entire group of soldiers flying all over the inside of the office, some even crashing through the walls, making large cracks or holes. Never before had she seen such magic. Her rapt attention was foolhardy, for in that split second, the unthinkable happened. In one stabbing motion, Right Hand plunged the stone shard into Sen-hi's wandering right eye, sending an unimaginable pain and torturous sensation of dark electricity coursing through her head, then through her body. She felt her world ending, without even being able to utilize her blade's ultimate attack, the legendary sword's successor sank to the floor, with the cackling, evil laughter of the dark man in the back of the room echoing throughout the office, throughout her head...as she slipped into a darkness unlike any she had ever experienced.

Sen-hi awoke surrounded in blinding light...lying down on a surface of white across from a robed figure. The figure beckoned her to rise, but Sen-hi hesitated. It was then she noticed something...something very odd. Sen-hi noticed that she had limited sight. Her hands searched her surroundings, trying to understand the reason for her limitation, when she finally remembered.

Slowly, fearfully, her hands searched her face, every crease, smooth outlines still there and then...she felt an eye patch where an eye should have been. Doubt set in almost immediately; she kept feeling the patch that was there, trying to understand how this could have happened with all her experience, all her skill. While she was doing this, she did not notice the figure now standing even closer to her. Instinctively, she went for her sword and un-sheathed it. The figure slowly uncovered the hood from its face and Sen-hi stood, confused and bewildered.

In front of her stood a man of somewhat pudgy stature, balding except for some receding hair surrounding the sides of his head. The features on his face and his complexion all pointed obviously to the fact that he was an Indian. He had a very calming, serene, yet commanding tone to his voice, "Lower your weapon, child. I mean you no harm. In fact, you have us to thank for healing your eye."

Sen-hi did not sheathe her sword, instead she stood in a fighting stance.

"Tell me, who are you, where am I and what happened to my eye?"

"I will gladly answer your questions, Sen-hi Sakeda, however, first I must ask you to give me your trust. It would be impossible for us to proceed without that very important action."

Sen-hi had been through too much to simply give her trust to someone...or something...she had never met before.

The figure must have felt this hesitation and offered a comforting sigh, "Sen-hi Sakeda, successor of the great and powerful legendary blade of Sakeda, your very namesake, you are engaged in yet another historic moment in man's existence and, such as it is not our place to constantly meddle in the affairs of fate, this particular situation has already been tarnished by the dark ones' involvement."

Sen-hi thought about what the figure was saying and recalled a similar encounter she had before the restoration of Emperor Meiji to the throne in her homeland.

"If this is another spiritual journey...I do not wish to know more. The last time I listened to the spirits, I almost died, lost my Father and was sent to this place...not here exactly, I do not know where HERE is, sent to America...betrayed by the very Emperor I personally helped install into power, surrounded by foreigners that hate me, insult me and treat me like an indentured servant."

"Captain Stephens and General Nelson do not think of you as a servant anymore, perhaps Nelson, yet they..."

"Surely you jest!" Sen-hi exploded, stamping her foot indignantly.

"If you are truly one of the spirits I grew to learn about, surely you have seen how 'Captain Stephens' treated me? He forced me to serve him! Forced me..."

"To learn English? Learn the culture and ways of this new country you are now a part of?" The figure interrupted, finishing her sentence.

"Tell me, Sen-hi, has Captain Stephens once forced you to personally serve him, as he does Miss Anne?"

Sen-hi hesitated, "Yes! He told me..."

"Has he once..." The figure interrupted again, "Actually made you physically do something FOR HIM? Not just threaten it, Sen-hi, did he make you do something physically you did not want to do?"

Sen-hi stood there, assailed by the eerie silence left between the two of them and thought hard. For all she could think of, she honestly could not think of one single thing the Captain actually made her do for him specifically. Most everything he asked of her was for her benefit or....at least it turned out to be that way after the fact. It was then she realized that she herself allowed her behavior. She permitted him to order her around.

Yet, "It doesn't make him perfect." She admitted, surveying her surroundings, which were bereft of anything. It all looked...white. No surfaces, nothing. "We don't need perfection, Sen-hi. We need someone who is, actually, imperfect."

"For what? You still haven't told me what this is about, who you are and why I am here...wherever here is?"

"I'm surprised this is still new to you, Sen-hi. Do you not remember all your experiences in Japan? With the old man? The one who turned out to be your Father?"

"How...how do you...?" Sen hi asked.

"You are asking me that...while standing here in these surroundings? Still, keeping you in suspense is not part of the plan. I am not a spirit. I am a monk. My name is Diego Guadalupe, Practiced Senior Elder of the Brothers of the Sacred Circle of the Earth Spirits. My tribal name, though, is Great Root. I am, as I am sure you already noticed, an...'Indian', as the whites call us."

"Why should I believe anything you say, then, Indian? I was just fighting your kind before you...kidnapped me?"

"My kind? I assure you, Sen-hi, those men...well, they were men... those dark ones you were fighting were not Indians...not Natives, as we call ourselves. They are merely Shadow Men. Minions of the dark one. They left their humanity and culture the moment they bonded with the stone."

"Stone? What stone?" A recollection of a stone near the Indian's leader, on the desk, came to her.

"He had a stone, I think. Still, Shadow Men? This must be a dream."

"No, my dear. No dream. This place you are in is a healing place. It is a place devoid of time or space, created by myself and some of my brothers in times of crisis to heal one of our own."

"What?"

"Sen-hi, I have much to tell you, but it does take up a great deal of energy and concentration to keep you here. I am going to release the healing circle and bring you back to the world, however, I must warn you, you will not be in the Fort and you will be surrounded by strange men, except for myself, which you will not recognize. Please do not attack anyone, they will not attack or harm you in any way. Do you understand?"

"Monk, as long as I am not touched or harmed, I assure you, you will not feel the sting of my blade."

Elder Diego smiled, "Release the hold." He said out loud. In an instant, the stark, white world around her collapsed like a fog and Sen-hi found herself thrust into yet another unknown place. This one had substance, smells and sights. She looked around and saw several men, in similar cloaks as Diego's, standing in a circle around her, Diego himself in the center. They were inside a large rounded structure, most definitely not in the Fort. It almost looked like the interior of a Pagoda, but with thatched roof instead of wooden frames and smoothed clay made out the floor. All around the room were masks of different designs and makes. Some she recognized as the avatars of deities native to Japan itself, others perhaps Chinese...Mongolian? The others were unknown to her, shapes of men seemingly morphed by parts of all manners of animals. Ears of an Elephant here, a beak of some bird there. There were mats on the floor, with cushions, used for meditation and rest, no doubt. In what she could only guess was the focal point of the room was a large wooden chair, accompanied by two figures that looked like statues. A Tengu Lion on one side and a large Eagle of unknown design on the other. The men all held out their hands in a gesture of peace. As promised, Sen-hi relaxed her stance, however, she did not divert her sight from the Monk, who had just taken a seat at the head chair in the room. The other Monks retreated slowly to their respective sitting places on the mats.

Sen-hi looked at the Monk inquisitively as he continued their conversation.

"We are an ancient order of spiritual men who do not exactly worship one particular deity. It's rather difficult to explain, but we... take missives from certain deities or their messengers and deliver them to specific parties that they are intended for. You met, or rather were related to, one of our brethren in Japan, your father, Masatoshi Sakeda."

"You are now the second person I have met in this country who knew of my Father."

"Who...oh, yes, the Captain, the Copy-Sword Master. It's, as they say, a small world now, Sen-hi. The edges of the map are no longer blurred. You were guided to your actions in Japan through your Father and, before you were sent to America, your Father sent a letter to us that you would make your way here somehow. Ever since that letter came..." The Monk took a letter out and handed it to her, "...we've been expecting your arrival."

Sen-hi handled the letter with utmost care, recognizing the handwriting on it almost immediately. It really was written by her Father. It read, "Fellow brethren of the Circle, I write to you under the gravest of circumstances. I am afraid that I will be drawn in to this civil war between my countrymen and the Shogun and his evil General Akushin Hiruma and fear my life will be forfeit before I see you again. As promised, I have instructed my oldest daughter, Sen-hi, in the ways of the sword and she has fulfilled the legacy of the Sakeda blade. I am sure she will be victorious in this fight and will, no doubt, make her way to America and, ultimately, to you. I implore you to offer her whatever services you deem appropriate and to keep her on the path of the righteous. She is a formidable warrior and even better human being. She is the perfect candidate for becoming the Sword of the Spirit."

Sen-hi looked up at the Monk, "Sword of...the Spirit?" The Monk nodded, "Yes, it is the name that is given to the chosen one who wields the ancient sword passed down by the Great Spirit to one of the 10 Houses of Spiritual Light in the world."

Sen-hi felt her head whirl in confusion, all this talk of spirits, power, houses, it was all too much for her. Still, she was the successor of the blade of Sakeda, a Samurai and warrior. She steeled herself and attempted to listen to everything this Monk had to say. Even if it meant she had to kill him after he spoke.

"The Great Spirit is the name given to the main deity that governs the spiritual power and energies that the Natives of this continent worship. He is a benevolent deity, capable of immense power, love, wisdom and punishment...to those that deserve it. We of this particular brotherhood serve him, however, there are other factions of our brotherhood located throughout the world, even in this very country, that serve other deities, they have other missions. Even though the different brotherhoods have different deities that they serve, we all have the exact same goal, the same main objective: to keep balance between the light and dark forces that exist on Earth. This our brotherhood has been doing ever since time immemorial. One of the first acts done to keep this balance was to build Houses around the world to contain different types of power, to help keep the balance. As it is with any power, though, the same sources that may exist to keep the power hidden and safe, also have sources that counter their existence to steal that power, to use it for their own nefarious means."

"You are speaking of the eternal battle between good and evil... as well as yin and yang. These are contrary beliefs, though. I am a Buddhist and, even though I am a warrior, I believe in keeping balance...", Sen-hi added.

"Through your sword?", the monk asked.

Sen-hi nodded.

"Exactly, Sen-hi. Your sword is a tool that you use to help keep the balance between the forces of light and dark. You, of course, work for the forces of good, of light, while others, like Akushin and this new evil one you encountered in the Fort, are of the forces of evil. It matters not what drove them to that evil, that they can only answer for themselves to their own gods. What matters is that they do work for those dark forces and that you, Sen-hi, are the one capable of stopping them...with that sword."

Sen-hi looked at her sword and tanto, both sheathed. She thought about what the Monk was telling her and wondered, "Still, it doesn't explain about my sword's legacy...the Sakeda blade. Did it come from one of these houses?"

"The blade itself is, remember, an extension of the person. A blade can be twisted, melted, destroyed...but the will of a person...their spirit... that is something that endures. Many years ago, your Father was going on a pilgrimage to a very ancient Buddhist shrine in Hokkaido, to pray for the safety of his...your...family legacy. While there, he stumbled upon a stone obelisk marker that drove him to a small, secluded temple hidden deep in the mountains. When he entered the temple, he saw writing all around him, foreign writing, and a glowing orb in the center of the main room in the Temple, encased in some kind of crystalline diamond." Sen hi nodded and the monk continued.

"He felt, he once wrote to us, compelled to come closer to the object and, before he knew it, he was holding the diamond. In his hands, it opened and the strange glow inside coursed through his entire body, instilling him with unbelievable power and insight. It was then he became the next successor of the secret...of the power of Sakeda."

"You speak as if Sakeda was something apart from him...?

The Monk smiled and continued, "Sakeda was not always your family name, my dear. Your Father may not have told you this, but the moment he inherited that power, he merged and became one with the great power of the spirit of Sakeda...the power of Justice. You, Sen-hi, are now the sole inheritor and successor of the Sakeda power...the power of Justice."

"Then...am I...invincible?", Sen hi asked.

"You, like us, are human. Justice, however, is an ideal, a thing immaterial, eternal, thus it never dies. As long as you adhere to your own true self, the truth of what you stand for shall never die, even if your body withers."

"That being said," Another Monk added, "You are not like other humans. Just as you inherited the skills and techniques of the Sakeda blade, your body 'inherited' the power of Justice. You will discover that a normal blade will have some difficulty in penetrating your skin, your reflexes, agility and strength are beyond that of man. Your sight in your injured right eye has now become enhanced, changed forever."

Monk Diego continued, "Correct, brother. When you learn to harness the ability, you will be able to access the sight of the Eagle flying high over the sky, as well as the sight of the wolf, who can see as clear as day during the night. You'll have the ability to see the slowness of the natural world, much as a bumblebee or flying insect does. Any sword skill set will be as simple for you to learn as it is simple for a baby to cry for its mother's milk. You'll be able to wield any weapon held in your hands, learning its secrets, techniques and fighting ways."

"This sounds incredulous.", Sen hi said. "How is it that these things were not known or made known to me before?"

"Your eye's new abilities were by accident, placed there as a tandem effect by the dark stone in combination with the spirit of Sakeda, protecting you from the dark powers. Every other ability...haven't you noticed by now how powerful you become when you fight?"

Sen-hi had to admit to herself, she always wondered why her fighting strength and power were so far above everyone else's. Even the most seasoned, the most experienced Samurai was little match for her. "You have helped clear many questions for me. Now, what of this present conflict I am finding myself within? What is to be my purpose here in this new land?"

"For that, my dear, you will have to listen a great deal longer. For the intentions of the dark forces and that of their new vessel, Raven Black, are far-encompassing and must be stopped...by you."

Sen-hi finally decided to sit and listen as Monk Diego and his brethren explained about Raven Black, the conflict between the Natives and the Americans, as well as her role in the fight.

CHAPTER EIGHT
TACTICS

Alone, Raven Black stood near the shore of the river, the same place, the same sights, smells and sounds he remembered from the vision he had so many months ago. In the middle of the river, his son, Right Hand, stood with his right hand raised. In his culture, a symbol of openness, a sign to him that his son was behind him all the way. This time, however, the vision would stray from the one he had before. This time, the river, the clear blue waters of the Little River so near his home, gradually turned dark blue, then black. The Mapiyan Leader dipped his hands in the water, which was now thick as tar. Quickly, he turned his attention to his son, who was now screaming. He was screaming because the tar was enveloping him, seeping into his skin, his eyes, until the Leader's son became as black as the tar water of the River. Raven Black attempted to come to his son's assistance, but he could not. He, too, was covered in the tar-like substance. Just as he was trying to make sense out of what he was experiencing, he noticed a third figure make an appearance over the river. It was that same girl he saw in the fort. This time, the girl's eyes were covered in mist and she was brandishing a bow and arrow. He saw that her sword was unsheathed, yet it hung, floating, to her side. Slowly, the girl raised her bow and arrow and it appeared as if she was pointing it at him.

Quickly, he lifted his hands to his heart, trying to cover his vital area, however, she did not shoot at him. Instead, she turned her bow and pointed it towards his son. Raven Black screamed out in protest, but it was too late. Already, the girl had loosed her arrow and it flew across the waters and right through his son's heart.

Suddenly, he awoke from his vision and the Mapiyan Leader was in a cold sweat. Again, he found himself unclear as to the meaning of his vision. It had changed little since the last one. The main difference seemed to be the tar and the girl. He took this as meaning that the battle between the Light Force's Champion and him was fast approaching. 'Why my son, then?', he wondered.

The Leader emerged from his tent, the meditative incense smell wafting from within.

"Bring me Shaman Spirit Bear." He commanded to one of his guards. The guard sped away on command as Black threw some more pieces of cut wood on the fire. Even during the day, the open prairie could be windy and unforgiving. Right Hand walked up to his father and the two exchanged a loving embrace. "Father, what troubles you?"

"Nothing, son. Just a bad dream I keep having."

Right Hand searched his Father's expression for a hint of a more detailed answer, but could not get anything else out of him. "The last three tribes of the Great Hunt have convened their assemblies. We shall know soon whether they will join us in our final assault against the white eye city."

"They had best decide soon and decide to join us.", Black added.

"I see no other way for them, my Father. The leaders of those tribes were, after all, fellow initiates that fought alongside you. It would be a great dishonor for them to refuse you now."

"True, but do not underestimate cowardice, son. It can stem in even the most stalwart, the most resolute heart. It takes a man of great power and ambition to overcome that fear of failure and rise above the squalor of humanity."

"We shall be victorious in the great struggle, Father. Their Champion is defeated, their forces beaten back, all that stands in our way is a port."

Raven Black took his son's words to heart and broke more firewood. "She was merely seriously wounded, son. I fear the corruption may not take its hold on her. I sensed too much doubt in her spirit towards the dark ones. She is, after all, a foreigner to these lands. It will take more than our new powers to make her see our way is righteous."

As the next pile of wood cracked in protest against the fire, the guard Black sent came back...alone.

"What is the meaning of this insult, warrior? Where is the Shaman of our tribe?!"

The guard quaked in mortal terror and responded in hesitation, "Sire...he...he is not here."

"What do you mean...he is not here?" Right Hand slowly inched his way closer to the warrior.

"Sir, he was not at his tent and when we went to look around the village, we found his horse gone and this..." The warrior handed a feather to Right Hand, who in turn handed it to his father.

Black's rage could be felt even within the warrior guard's heart. He quivered even more as he continued, "...was all we found in the place of the horse." The guard shook in fear, the light in his eyes escaping with every gush of blood dripping from the wound that was just caused by Right Hand's lightning-quick attack to his chest.

Black tossed the feather to the floor, unaffected by one of his tribe member's death, "We need to focus on getting the other tribes to join us. If the Shaman has turned traitor, he will no doubt inform the white eye of our plans. Hitch up the horses, the new weapons and all the stones, then rally the rest of the men and women of the tribes, keep a small force here to draw the enemy's attention, while the rest of us move the main force somewhere more strategic. Inform our mutual 'friend' of the situation and see what new information, if any, he has to offer us of his previous slavers and their fortifications and armaments in San Francisco's main headquarters, the Presidio."

Right Hand nodded his affirmation and sped off. Raven Black thought long and hard about the vision he just had. Without his old friend, Shaman Spirit Bear, he could not hope to decipher its true meaning.

General Nelson put aside another page of scribbles and diagrams brought forth to his tent, ideas of attacks and strategies that had been discarded. The recent defeat and loss of Fort Francisco and Commander Reese was a very serious hit against the US Army. Captain Stephens rushed in with more details of the Indians' movements and he brushed it aside, pointing to the pile of identical paperwork that he had been given by his Lieutenants in the field. "We were sorely mistaken when we decided to go up against this enemy. This is unlike any Indian encounter we have ever come across."

"True, sir. Which is why we need to re-think every single scenario and plan of attack before we put it to effect."

"Don't get snide, Captain. I am well aware of our losses, both in death and..in...whatever they are now that some of our own soldiers had been turned. We had no way of knowing that the enemy had magic in their arsenal. At least not to the level they were wielding it."

"Then, sir, perhaps it is time we add some...magic to our arsenal."

"No, the weapons are not ready. We'll have to rely..."

"On what...a samurai girl and her skill? Because that is the only difference we had in the last battle, sir."

"She helped save hundreds of our men, Captain."

"But we ended up losing hundreds upon hundreds. And we ended up losing her!"

"Not so.", the General said.

Captain Stephens' look of confusion stayed with him as the General explained, "She was taken away from the battle by a monk that contacted me some time ago. I cannot divulge their identity, they exist in a completely immune and separate form from our regimental forces, yet their authoritative reach is grand. Enough so that within a day of Sen-hi's disappearance, I received a missive from a Government agent of her whereabouts and return."

"Sir, quite frankly, this is the most ridiculous thing I have heard yet. It's one thing for me to stomach the existence of magical items, magical people, even amazing technological achievements... but you are telling me that this woman...a foreigner...has been given that kind of high-level access, to our government, that she is immune to our orders and that we're just...to accept her vanishing from an important part of the battle and her eventual return? Just like that?"

"Yes, Captain. Just like that.", the General smartly responded, pointing to the tent's doorway, where Sen-hi now stood, holding a rope tied to an Indian in ceremonial garb. "And I bring you a gift from the great beyond, Captain."

Later that night, the three sat down to their dinner and discussed what Sen-hi had experienced. "Are you going to need a special unit for the mission from the monks?"

Sen-hi looked at the General and nodded. "Just a handful of your most trusted and skilled warriors may accompany me. Anymore would be a hindrance."

"What about retaliation?"

"We are, of course, to expect it, given the details of the mission, however, one of the men you are to give me must have a specialty to assist us with that problem."

The General smiled knowingly, "I see what you're getting at. Crafty, crafty there, missy. I know just the soldier."

"Hold on," Captain Stephens raised his hand in protest, "You mean to say that you're just going to waltz in to Raven Black's head tent or whatever those redskins call it...kidnap his second-in-command and just...walk out of there? And you're going to do it with maybe five men? Are you both insane?"

"Captain, I am surprised at you. I personally have seen enough of this young lady's skill and expertise on the battlefield, both with my own eyes and through my men's eyes, to know that she is perfectly suited for this extractive exercise. In fact, I would highly suggest, milady, you take the good Captain here as your number two."

Stephens blanched at the thought and looked at Sen-hi, who had the most satisfied smirk on her face.

"As you order, General." Sen-hi responded, with a proud tone to her voice.

"Now, on to the business of the um...gift you brought us." The General nodded over to one of his guards and they left the room.

"Yes, sir. After my conversation with Monk Diego, I was escorted to an adjoining hut where an Indian was waiting, along with one of the others that I was speaking with. I then..."

"Wait, 'others'? Others, what? Who are these people she was with and who is this monk? Why haven't I heard of them, sir?" the Captain asked.

"I already explained, Captain, they are a special..."

"Yes, yes, special attachment, separate from the government under their own authority. And, what, we are supposed to simply follow their 'suggestions' blindly? Sir, forgive my disrespect, but, aren't you being a tad cavalier about all this? And since when do we ever allow a woman to take command of a unit or to brief us on anything other than the condition of our doilies and uniforms?!"

General Nelson could see that Stephens was visibly shaken by all these new 'changes' that had happened so suddenly and without his approval or even consideration. "Walk with me for a moment, Captain. Sen-hi, please wait."

The Captain followed his commander outside the tent and the two just stood there while the General laid out the terms. "Captain, what age are we living in now?"

"Sir?"

"The age, what age is this? Surely not the Stone or Bronze Age, correct?"

"Sir, I do not see the relevance of..."

"Captain, we just finished fighting a war of immense scope. You may have heard of it...the Civil War? We are just now getting back on our feet as a nation and are reconstructing most of our country. Now, hitch on a brand new adversary in the form of these damn redskins and we're in a fine mess. We're low on provisions, ammunition, equipment and, most of all, men. Quite frankly, we can't spare a single solitary soul. The loss at Fort Francisco especially speaks tragic volumes towards the situation. We can ill afford another war, let alone massive struggle in our state. Can you imagine our overseas enemies looking here now? Why, they'd pick us off as easy as a gnat on a catatonic horse! We cannot afford to be beggars in our opinions of those who wish to offer us aid, especially ones that are as skilled as that young lady in there. Now, I am well aware of the breach in protocol and in etiquette that her presence in this man's army presents, however, I am also willing to ignore it...albeit temporarily... until this conflict with those thievin' bastards is complete. After all the smoke is clear, after the head of the Mapiya is captured and brought to justice for his crimes, you may do with her what you wish. You won't hear one word of protest out of me."

Captain Stephens thought long and hard about what the General said. His eyes followed his Commander as he walked away to continue the strategic detail. Perhaps, he thought, perhaps he would just play along for now. Until the struggle is over. Yes, he thought. When the struggle is finished, he knew exactly what he would do with this... General.

Shaman Spirit Bear's new surroundings were as foreign to him as the girl he shared his room with. The white eye army treated him far nicer than he expected, they set him up in a small military housing tucked well within the base's interior, along with some quaint amenities, bed light, even a plate with some food. The food was odd, it had a smoky smell to it, cooked and seasoned.

In the room with him was the woman who delivered him, a young foreign girl with a strange eye named Sen-hi. "Do you understand me, young one?" Sen-hi's raised eyebrow made the Shaman ask again, "I have something important to tell you, child and I pray you can understand my words. I may not be an American, but I do speak their language passably well." Sen-hi slowly placed her hand on her weapon and motioned for him to continue. Shaman Spirit Bear pointed to the large bag that he brought with him, which was near Sen-hi. She very carefully passed it to him and he patted it, affectionately. "When my old friend Proud Eagle, the man you now know as Raven Black, approached me to give him my blessing to become the tribal chief, I knew then he was up to something sinister."

"Why help him, then, Gaijin?"

The Shaman eyed Sen-hi inquisitively, not sure what to make of her strange word.

She responded, "It means 'savage' or 'barbarian' in my language. It is not meant as a term of offense, more of a literal term. Now, again, why help him?"

Shaman Spirit Bear pointed towards the door, "Your friends, we call them 'White Eye' because they are blind to the world around them, they have made us this way. Over the many settings of the sun, the many waxes and wanes of the moon, my people have been forced out of our hunting grounds, our homes, by the White Eye. They came here in their great canoes, their ships, speaking of friendship and compromise and, while their leader, the one called 'President Grant', extends peaceful proposals and land grants, their arm of might, the army, seems to contradict his edicts and swallows our hunting lands, moves us to 'protected settlements', all in the name of expansion, something they call 'manifest destiny'." The Shaman paused for a moment and realized that Sen-hi was still listening, yet the look on her face had changed...to one of anger. "You mean to say to me that this was the reason they are at war with your people? Manifest Destiny? Expansion?"

"Yes, young one, I..."

"Don't believe everything he tells you, Sen-hi." The two turned to see the General enter the room, eyeing the Shaman closely.

"General, did you know this treachery he speaks of?", Sen-hi asked.

"Sen-hi, there is no treachery. Everything can be misconstrued, misunderstood and warped to fit the side of the one telling the story.", he responded.

"How?!", she asked.

"Well, until today you were fully on the side of the United States Government...were you not?" Sen-hi paused and nodded.

"This Indian is angry at us because his lands, the lands of his ancestors, are being taken and repurposed to serve the needs of the American people.", the General stated.

"Centuries of undisturbed wilderness, spiritual growth and generations of living tribes, your people are destroying it in the pulling of a trigger.", the Shaman spat.

"What he is not telling you," General Nelson responded, "...is that his people were on the brink of starvation, even eventual extinction. Your 'generations', as you called them, had been exhausting the resources you claimed to protect so fervently. The bison had been running unchecked and un-culled, their population would have eventually become so out-of-control that your tribes would have had no choice but to kill off the extraneous elements of the breed. What about your internal strife, Indian?"

"I am Shaman Spirit Bear, White Eye."

"Fine, I'll call you by your name...if you call me by mine, deal?" The Shaman hesitantly agreed and the General continued, "As I was saying, Shaman..."

"Hold, General. You speak of these out-of-control things, these elements producing chaos around us, having us brought to the brink of extinction, but what you fail to understand is that this is an end already seen by our people. We were and are prepared for the end... even if it is a horrific, bloody, violent end. You, however, your kind, your people, you were not foreseen by any of us."

"Your monks...your 'Shamans'...they didn't see the Americans, the white men, coming?" Sen-hi inquired, taking a seat finally.

"Some spoke only of vague rumors. An unknown force, much like a wave, would wash upon our shores and wipe out everything that once was the land of the free."

"Rather bold of you to speak of this as a land of the free. We just finished a bloody, brutal war and freedom...a type of freedom, of ownership, was just lost."

"Yes, or won, depending on the perception, General.", the Shaman said.

For the first time in the conversation, Sen-hi felt confused. "There was a war here? Separate from the battle your two peoples are currently embroiled in?"

"Yes, Sen-hi. The white eye had a rather long and costly Civil War between the Northern States and Southern States, it lasted for many years and many good men were sacrificed during the war."

"Sacrificed is the wrong word, Indian. They volunteered to serve the Union..."

"And Confederacy, General.", the Shaman added.

"What was that war about?", Sen-hi asked.

"Many will tell you it was about slavery, about the status of the Africans and whether their taskmasters could actually own them or not. There was more to it, though. Many States wanted the right to regulate their own taxes and tariffs, apart from the Federal Government, it's all rather technical. The point is, we had several forts in the main city of San Francisco that had to be re-purposed from the former war against the Mexicans to use for the War of the States."

"You people are a warlike bunch.", Sen-hi said.

"They are a savage race, Sen-hi." The Shaman nodded, yet, Sen-hi matched his gaze, even with her one eye and contended, "I like war, Shaman." The Shaman was visibly shocked by her response and slowly shook his head in defeat.

The General smiled victoriously, "She's a Samurai, Indian. That means she was bred in battle, lives to serve in war. We're wasting time, though, I can tell you more later and within friendlier locations. Shaman, I must ascertain why you agreed to come to us. Are you willing to give us information about your Commander, his plan of attack? Anything that can be of use?"

"General, the leader of our people, Raven Black, as he now calls himself, rarely ever makes his plans known and, when he does, he only tells his second-in-command, Right Hand, who is also his son. I was never informed of his strategy, only of the outcome. The information I come bearing, though, is of supreme importance."

"Very good, on with it.", the General demanded.

The Shaman bristled in frustration and stated simply, "I will only tell her. This information is not for unworthy ears, I am afraid."

"No, Shaman, you are the one who should be afraid if you do not tell me all you know. Right now." The General uncoiled his whip and let it hang loose on his side.

The Shaman saw this action and shrugged, "No manner of torture will pry this information from me. It was entrusted to me by the Spirits and I am more fearful of eternal torment for telling you than I am of your whip." The General grimaced at the Shaman's stubbornness and turned sharply to regard Sen-hi. "Now, listen well, girl. You will relay every single bit of information this prisoner gives you back to me, word for word. You are to leave nothing out. Do not let him sway you with pretty stories of tribal rights, Indian natural law and any other mumbo jumbo. You are a soldier in this man's army now and you have sworn allegiance to President Ulysses S. Grant. Do you understand,

Samurai?" Sen-hi nodded slowly and he summarily left the chamber. She then turned her attention back to her captive and was surprised to see him unafraid, in fact, putting more wood to the fireplace.

"When my old friend, once called Elder Proud Eagle, came to me and asked me to help him ascend to the status of sole tribal leader, I must confess that there was a part of me that knew it was the wrong thing to do."

"Then why did you perform the ceremony of ascension?", she asked.

"As I mentioned, young one, he was my friend. More than that, I think. When you live in a tribe, my dear, you live like a family. Your tribe *is* your family. It is why we call each other brother and sister. Every person in the village has a purpose, a role to play. They fulfill the purpose with all their body, heart and spirit. It's because of this that it troubled...still troubles me that my friend of so many years can so completely accept and become the pawn of the root of evil."

"The potter can be perfect, Shaman, the clay can have perfect shape, proportion and volume and still turn out flawed. It may take days, months, even years but even the most resolute sculpture can develop cracks until, ultimately, even that 'perfect man' turns into a different animal altogether."

The Shaman smiled, "I had my doubts at first when you approached me, saying that the Monks sent you, but now I know you are the right one to finish this."

"Continue." Sen-hi urged, handing him another piece of splintered wood. The Shaman sighed, placing the wood on the fire gently. The wood groaned, fractured further in protest and the fire grew slowly in unison. "Black has a grand plan for the tribes, Sen-hi Sakeda. He plans to attack the main port here in San Francisco, The Presidio. Before he does that, he plans to take as many forts along the way as he can."

"How does he plan on doing that?", she prodded.

"The answer is not surprising, really. It will happen the same way he took the last Fort. With a massive army of Shadow Men." Sen-hi was about to ask when Shaman Spirit Bear raised his hand in polite interruption.

"Think, young one. Think to your last battle. You encountered the Shadow Men of Black already. Your General has also."

"Is that what they are? Shadow...men? What does that mean?", she asked.

"When you were stabbed, you were stabbed with a very unique weapon, were you not?"

"I could only see it for a brief instant before impact. A rock of some sort. The Monks say I still have a small piece of it lodged in my 'good eye'."

Sen-hi rubbed her eye patch, part of her missed having two eyes she could use all the time, the other part felt fortunate for the gifts she was now given and that, at least, she hadn't lost her sight completely.

The Shaman admired the girl's tenacity in the face of such overwhelming magic. His curiosity and admiration for the Monks' techniques got the better of him and he humbly asked, "May...I see it, Sen-hi?"

Sen-hi shrugged and lifted the patch, revealing her eye for the first time since her training at the Monks' abbey. The Shaman slowly inched towards Sen-hi, making sure to show her his hands raised at all times. She did not appear intimidated nor wary, but she was, he knew, always prepared to fight. The eye was indeed unique in appearance and design. Yes, the Shaman decided, design was perhaps the best descriptive term. Her left eye was still a strong, yet not too deep brown while her right was a penetrating, almost glowing, silver. The blackened center had a small, diagonal purple scar upon it. The white of it was filled with sheen silver coloring, almost rippling with electrical energy. As a Shaman, he had a special connection with nature and the world around him. His master had taught him how to commune with the forces of power in nature and he felt the pulsing, limitless potential in that one eye. He wanted to search more, for answers and meaning, but he saw Sen-hi's facial muscles twitch slightly and decided to help her put her patch back on.

"It hurts if exposed for too long, I gather." He concurred, sitting back down in his chair.

Sen-hi nodded, "I still have to train more. It takes a measure of focus to control and for now, I can only master less than a handful of animals."

"Amazing. So the stone gave you..."

"The spirits gave me this power, Shaman, not the stone." Sen-hi interrupted, tapping the patch with her hand.

"Of course, the stone must act as a conduit of sorts. I can teach you the next steps, if you are willing to trust me."

Sen-hi put up her hand, "First, we must know Raven Black's exact strategies, Shaman."

"But you are the Champion of..."

"I am Sen-hi Sakeda, the successor of the Blade of Sakeda, I am the Sword of Justice, yes. But I am also human and have been given the honor and privilege of a title in this country's army. I am sure the General told you that I am a Samurai?"

The Shaman sighed in defeat. She wasn't ready yet. "Yes, he mentioned something like that, I seem to recall."

"As a Samurai, I live to serve my Master. So, while I accept my role as the Light's Champion, I do not fully understand that role, nor do I fully understand this gift I have been given. I first must act on what I already know. I will stop this onslaught, this massive continuing attack of Black's and when I am satisfied he is at a weak point, then I will give you my undivided attention."

"Sen-hi, how do you expect to defeat Raven Black or his forces if you allow so many outside forces to control your actions?", he asked.

"Nothing controls me, Shaman, except my hunger for Justice at all costs.", she responded.

"That, my dear, could be your biggest strength or greatest flaw. I will tell you all I know of his strategy, but you must first know one thing that I would urge you impart to your superiors."

"What?", she asked.

"Raven Black is not acting alone. Yes, he has his Shadow Army, but that is only part of his plan. He also has someone working for him with intimate knowledge of your army's inner workings. This man joined the tribe just before the taking of the Fort and I am afraid his treachery is just beginning."

"What? Who is he?", she asked.

"An acquaintance of yours, I believe. He spoke of you often..."

Sen-hi could feel her skin crawl, her hairs on her arms bristled in anticipation as the Shaman uttered the name, "Lieutenant Robert Macarthur."

Raven Black sat sulking in his chair, listening to the innermost details being divulged by his newfound 'ally', former Lieutenant, Robert Macarthur. "Once you get your main forces past the harbor and into the main receiving yard for the docks, it should be short work to breach the Presidio's northern gates.", Macarthur pointed out.

"If what you say is true, we will be mounting an offensive against a thousand, possibly more, heavily armed and skilled soldiers, Macarthur." Right Hand doubted, scanning very carefully the layout provided by the former Lieutenant.

"The fort looks impenetrable except by sea and we are not a sea-faring people. The enemy will know this and provide a great deal of support to cover their entrance with great warships.", Right Hand said.

"Which is why we will not attack the Presidio yet, son.", Black stated.

Right Hand turned to account for his father's words, as he continued, "We will first take Fort Harrison, the nearest fortification to the Presidio. From there, we can mount a flanking attack."

"Flanking? Father, there is no opening towards the Presidio's back.", Right Hand pointed out.

"There will be. You see, even now I have intelligence from my imprisoned brethren that they are creating an area with which we will make our move. The Americans will have no idea how or when their largest naval port on these shores is being infiltrated and taken over by the time we overcome the meager might of Fort Harrison."

"And what of the Champion, Father?", Right Hand asked.

"I wouldn't worry too much about her. She is ill-equipped to face me now. And without her skills, how will the white eye hope to win against the power of the stone?"

The General and Captain Stephens concluded their meeting, both feeling more confident this latest strategy would not fail. Both men sat down in Stephens' smoking room, while Miss Anne dutifully served her famous sweet crackers and ginger ale. "Master Stephens?" Miss Anne asked, shifting her uneasy eyes between the two men in front of her. "Yes, Miss Anne?", the Captain asked.

"Where is Sunny? I haven't seen hide nor hair of her in a while. Did you send her away? Did I teach her right?"

Captain Stephens smiled, "Yes, Miss Anne. You taught her English very well. I did not send her off, she is actually in a different role now. You may not ever see her again. I trust that will not be a serious problem?"

"Oh no, Master Stephens! Hell, the girl was right trouble from the start! Always talkin' about fightin' and swords and this n' that. Shoot, I'm glad she's gone!"

The Captain noticed a small tear escape his servant's eye and called it to her attention, "Your tears betray you, Miss Anne. You do miss her!" The two shared a good laugh and Miss Anne excused herself to the kitchen.

"Should be a good dinner tonight, sir. We'll be havin' roast chicken with all the trimmins!", she said upon her exit.

"Oh, what's the occasion?", he asked.

"You're home, sir." She said, flatly. Stephens and the General exchanged looks, knowing how serious absence in the line of duty can take on a family, friends...even staff.

"Fine house servant you got there, Stephens. How did you manage to keep her after the war? I would've thought the coloreds were all freed?", the General inquired.

"She is free, sir. She is a well-paid, well-taken-care-of servant. I offered her freedom well before the war started, but she insisted on staying on staff. I honestly don't think she knows how to do anything else. She's been the servant of my family since before my Father died."

"Damn fine commitment, if you ask me.", he added.

"Yes, sir." Stephens shifted uncomfortably and took a long sip before exhaling, letting his discomfort known.

"Yes, out with it, Stephens. What are you on about now? Not still the Samurai girl, I trust?", the General demanded.

"No sir, actually, it's about...your arm." For the first time since the Battle at Little River, The General uncovered his cloak to reveal a marvel of steam-powered engineering. In the place of his right arm, there was a working, gold-plated, mechanical arm. The General willed it to rise and fall, even stop mid-way.

"All motions are at my command. I can open and close my fist, point, use all fingers as a...normal person can."

"Astounding." Stephens awed, finding it hard to take his eyes off of it. "Will this be the new arms for our other injured.."

"Oh, I doubt it, Stephens." The General interrupted, shifting the cup to his right arm. "This sort of thing is reserved for those of us in the army with distinction." Captain Stephens knew that was just a pretty way of saying that only men with a special place in the force would get the hardware.

"I wasn't there when it happened, sir. How did this come to be?", the Captain asked.

"I was called in to the fray after one of our siege tanks became incapacitated by an unknown force. Upon hearing the impossible news, I mounted my horse and galloped at a furious pace to the assault plane. When I arrived, I saw a rising plume of black smoke and char marks on the ground where the tank was. Around the ground, I saw men lying down, some dead, others wishing they were so. I rushed off my horse to the nearest fallen soldier. He was coughing up blood, his face a blackened, bloody mess. Stephens... it was horrid."

Stephens pat his back, only to have it waved off.

"No, no. As Officers in this man's army, we need to be above these human emotions, Stephens."

"Sir...we are human." Stephens replied, eyeing the General very worryingly.

The General shrugged and continued, "The soldier gave me some valuable information then. He told me that the Savages had some airborne weapons at their disposal. These floating behemoths would unleash a volley of flaming bombardments that would have crashed through the unyielding metal on my tanks! Can you imagine the sheer force behind such an incendiary device? As I lay there, straddling the dying soldier's head against my arm, a new volley of death rained down near us and the next thing I knew, I woke up in my tent, attended by my personal medic and hand-selected rune engineer, the professor. You can thank them for my new arm."

"Sir...what happened to the...", the Captain asked.

"Stephens, not everyone can get this new power. You best be glad you are among the better men in my command. Not to worry, if anything were to happen, I would make sure you wouldn't leave us so quickly." Captain Stephens leaned back on his sofa, thinking long and hard on the General's story and his new appendage. He wondered if, perhaps, he may be on the wrong side of this conflict for the first time in his career. He also felt very envious of his former servant, no, fellow warrior Sen-hi's, ignorance and distance from General Nelson.

CHAPTER NINE
THE HUNT

Sen-hi and her companion, Shaman Spirit Bear, had been traveling by horse for a week now, stopping only to make camp and rest for the next leg of their journey. The animals in this land were different from Japan. There were some consistencies, some of the Cranes looked similar, as did the insects and some livestock.

Her concentration was broken by a bird call, somewhere above. *"When you learn to harness the ability, you will be able to access the sight of the Eagle flying high over the sky, as well as the sight of the wolf, who can see as clear as day during the night."*

Sen-hi slowly pulled up her eye patch, revealing her once-normal right eye. Now, however, she would only be able to use it as a specific tool. It took some getting used to, experimenting with small animals at first, honing in on a squirrel as it scampered up a tree...as she scampered up a tree. She later would practice on larger targets: A fox or some form of large feral cat. The flying animals were the hardest to focus on. They were always in motion, never in the same place twice.

Reaching within herself, she found the quiet darkness that existed in her right eye. The darkness, however, lasted for a moment. Then, she saw and felt a dizzying pull, through a whirlpool of confusing imagery and sounds. Suddenly, she was seeing a different vantage point. She could see what the bird was seeing. The tops of the tree line lined up beneath her body, the feathers flapping amidst the fleeting air, her wings caressing the cool breeze that she was now in control of. She was no longer just seeing through this animal's eyes. Sen-hi was the bird. The feel of the air on her face was very different than what she felt while on the back of a trotting horse. It was a visceral, primal feeling. This new face showed her that this new gift granted her much more than just sight and she loved every moment of it. Then, just as she honed into the bird's journey, she left it. Her head swam with dizziness and slight nausea, a feeling she hoped would subside with greater practice.

During their trek, Sen-hi often marveled at the awe-inspiring natural beauty and splendor of this country, this 'America' she had recently become a citizen of. The ceremony was rather lackluster, she recalled. Just before they departed, General Nelson and Captain Stephens acted as witnesses and the swearers of oath as she administered her allegiance to the Constitution of the United States of America and her newfound fealty to America's Manifest Destiny. The Shaman was also present at the oath ceremony and there had been something nagging at him since then, something he wondered.

"Sen-hi, now that you are a citizen...may I ask you something?"

"Certainly."

"Why? Why are you a citizen?"

Sen-hi slowed her horse to a slow trot. "I felt it necessary in order to complete the mission at hand, Shaman. What is the reason behind the question?"

"I find it difficult to comprehend how you, a Princess of a Royal House, child of a country torn apart by foreign intervention, tribal warfare and internal fiscal catastrophe could possibly swear fealty to an imperialist nation like this one? Especially after the story you told me of how they treated you when you arrived."

"Shaman...I am a Samurai. I live to serve. I did what I felt was necessary. That is all I will say at this time."

The Shaman, not really understanding, but deciding to forego any further questions, shifted the cantle on his saddle slightly. The two companions came to a fork in the road, where a sign with slightly faded, etched words read, "Western Bridge" on one arrow-shaped marker and "Mountain River Pass" on another.

Shaman Spirit Bear pointed towards the Mountain River Pass

marker, indicating their next turn. Sen-hi urged her horse, whom she lovingly named 'Toshiro', onward and the Shaman followed.

"This next part of our journey will seem the longest, but in actuality we will arrive at our final destination in 6 moons."

"Then it will be short of a week. This is a very long country you inhabit, Shaman. How sure are you that your allies and friends will still be alive by the time of our return?", she asked.

"There is never a guarantee, young one. There is a possibility all of the men you met may be dead upon your return, as it may be certain Raven Black..." The Shaman paused, collecting his emotions before he continued, "...may be certain that the new leader of my people may have actually conquered yet another white eye fort."

"Why do you keep referring to the Americans as 'white eye'? Why do you not call me that name?", she inquired.

"Firstly, you do not inhibit the traits. Secondly, the name is given to them that do not see the truth behind nature and life, as I stated to you earlier. These Americans destroy all they touch, Sen-hi Sakeda. Do you not see it? Every piece of land they conquer, they change to suit them, they cut timber, build houses and mutilate animals without utilizing the entire animal. They treat nature as a whore. You do not see this?"

"I see many things, Shaman. I simply choose to help nature and life in my own way."

"Hence you are not a white eye. Yet they are."

"Why are you here with me on this journey, then?", she said flatly.

"I am here for you, not them. Sen-hi, you are the Spirit of Justice incarnate. I, as a Shaman, serve the Spirits. I suppose you can say...I am your Samurai!"

The two shared a laugh, a rare event between them.

"I serve an important role, both as your guide, as well as your mentor in the world of spirits we are about to encounter. These roads we are on do not just go to the forest and mountains, Sen-hi. Those are also homes to spirits, monsters and other creatures that man has long since forgotten.", he explained.

"We have ancient forests in Japan as well. Many times I have ventured into them, encountering kodama, wolf spirits and many things that would make even you shudder in fear.", she said.

"I have seen much in my time here, I think I will be less fearful than you think.", he smiled.

Sen-hi stopped her horse and motioned her companion to quiet. Ahead of them, the road turned to mostly dirt and narrowed slightly as it went into the forest ahead. The wind moved the fallen leaves across their horses' hooves. The road ahead seemed to yawn and stretch further than their eyes would allow them to see. Noises, faint and strange, gnawed at Sen-hi's warrior instinct. "Weapons out." To her command, Sen-hi's sword unsheathed. The Shaman slowly took out his dagger and the two urged their horses onward, slowly and cautiously searching their surroundings. Without warning, a rustle in the bushes revealed its intention. An ear-splitting whistle and then an arrow flew just past Sen-hi, sticking itself on a tree across from them.

"We're under attack! Dismount and defend yourself, Shaman!", Sen-hi cried out.

The two companions immediately dismounted and clapped their horses to safety. The unseen assailants loosed more arrows, however, Sen-hi deftly parried them with her sword's amazing speed. From both sides, the hidden attackers made themselves known. The Shaman lifted his dagger, blocking a spear meant for his head. The two acted as an organized, experienced duo, fighting off what turned out to be 5 men and 1 still unseen archer in the shadows of the trees. Still, these attackers were just as organized. Sen-hi's own battle was fierce. The two adversaries parried, dodged and jumped apart, almost after every attack. They read each other's attacks well, calculating and planning each stroke before it was attempted. "Sen-hi, these are not ordinary bandits! Be on your guard!", the Shaman's voice carried through the fray.

"I know how to defend, Shaman! Look to your own flank!", the Samurai shouted, kicking a hard stone across the head of an oncoming attacker to her companion's backside, thereby stunning them.

Sen-hi's enemy took that opportunity to reposition themselves.

"You are indeed skilled, bandit. But you face a unique opponent holding this blade."

"Shut it, I'm a girl too!", the bandit spat.

Sen-hi was taken aback by this admission, parrying another sword fall by her enemy.

"Sakeda Ryu, Karakuri no Ken." In a blinding arc, Sen-hi brought down the blade in front of her with such force, that the wind between her and the girl dis-placed them from each other and knocked the girl backwards several feet.

"The hell? You a monster or somethin'?", the girl bandit asked.

"I am the successor of the legendary blade of Sakeda, daughter of the last house of Ikeda-haji, heralded by Masotoshi Sakeda, forthwith of my namesake. You, my attacker, are bested."

The young girl looked Sen-hi over and smirked. She slowly sheathed her sword and called out, "Stand down! Bring them into the main camp."

As the rest of the so-called bandits stopped their attacks, the girl motioned for Sen-hi and the Shaman to follow her down a faded dirt road off the beaten path they were already on.

"These two must be the ones Bright Dusk mentioned. Put away your legendary blade. Come, Successor of the Sakee Sakee, forthwith of what God gives the hell. We have much to discuss."

Some 100 yards off the road they were traveling, the cobblestone path ended and there was nothing but a copse of trees surrounding a well-hidden area. Some more distance took them to what looked like an abandoned village.

"Left over from the Civil War, some abandoned Union base, we think. We use it as our home away from...well, what we used to call home. I think you and your friend over there will fit in nicely." Sen-hi took in her surroundings and marveled at how these people took this abandoned base and made it their own. Some of the old houses were made into armories or smithies, there was a bonfire in the middle of the village, and Sen-hi understood already how few strategists there really were in this group. As they approached the center of the site, a man, cloaked in the robes of a tribal chieftain, stepped out of one of the houses.

The Shaman looked confused, stealthily moving his hand to his dagger for precaution.

"Our leader, Bright Dusk.", the girl bandit presented.

The cloaked man motioned for the two companions to join him inside his house. The interior was adorned with heads of different game animals, with a fire pit in the middle. It was well-arranged, looking more like a combination of the inside of a Sioux Tipi and American Cabin. The 'bandits' entered one after another, their demeanor changed, Sen-hi noticed, from adversarial to simply cautious.

"Your decor is impressive, 'Bright Dusk'. Are you a Sioux Brother?", Spirit Bear inquired.

The Bandit Leader, Bright Dusk, smiled at the Shaman's question, motioning to the woven, patterned blanket hanging over his chair.

"My Mother was a Sioux Chief-wife. She spirited me away from our village during a white eye attack." He flashed pained eyes at one of the bandits, an American, by the looks of him, Sen-hi thought.

"She took me to live in the wilderness by herself, best as she could. She soon discovered a woman alone could not survive this harsh land and she left me to the white eyes for education. At the age of reckoning, or I believe it is 18 by your American standards, I completed my education and set out to join the militia. Being a Native, they would only place me as a caller, someone to speak positively about the re-education programs for the 'Indians'. It was there I met Lieutenant Chris Steele over here."

The American in the group nodded, tapping his weapon, a flintlock blunderbuss, with pride.

"Steele and I became good friends and it wasn't until later that I discovered that he was a Private during that raid on my mother's village. Instead of hating him for being a part of it, we decided that we would leave the white eye settlement and build one of our own, with free thinkers, brothers and sisters of strong upbringing. That is what you are sitting in now, we call it New Liberty. It is populated by a wide variety of settlers, Natives, Americans, even foreign visitors like yourself, girl. We had become used to the customary incursion by neighboring Native Tribes, trying to take our home. We are on the border between Sioux and Mapiya lands. Tensions have escalated over recent months ever since the border markers were changed by the President. My people's villages have been raided and sacked on a terrifyingly frequent basis. I had scouts sent out to gather word and talk had reached us of a new larger conflict between the new General of the Military here, Nelson and the new leader of the Mapiya, a mystery to us, Raven Black. These two monsters have devious plans in mind and must be stopped at all costs. When my scout from the monks of Spirit Rock to the South reached us, they informed us that two visitors would be coming this way. A warrior and healer. The way the scout described the monk's words, I was expecting someone with more experience under their belt; And, to be honest, I would have preferred for you to be one of my people. But, if there is one thing isolation has taught us, it is that we are to be patient and grateful for the gifts of the Spirits. Tell us, then, who are you and why were you sent this way?"

Sen-hi paused, trying to ascertain both the truth from this man's words, as well as the general aura of the people around her. She marveled at the diversity of these people. Brothers in arms, yes, even sisters at that. Even amongst the Meiji Restorative Coalition, the operatives and soldiers were chosen with great care. She was, in fact, the only woman who had been given the great honor of being involved in the attack on Edo Castle.

"I am Sen-hi Sakeda, daughter of Masotoshi Sakeda and inheritor of the legendary blade of Sakeda-Ryu. I have had words and dealings with both of those men you mentioned. General Nelson recently sent me on a mission to find dissidents of his army and...take care of them."

The 'bandits' immediately bristled with renewed apprehension, their weapons drawn closer as a precaution.

"At no time did I ever have any intention of blindly following his orders." She responded to their tension, "For months, I have played the 'foolish servant', listening to his selfish prattling, boasts and threats. Purposefully acting demure and submissive. It is essential, of course, to gauge your opponent before you defeat them, know them intimately so as to best see their weaknesses."

The Shaman was speechless before this admission. All this time he had thought her to be an unfeeling machine of war, capable of manipulation by the slightest twinge of emotion from the right type of man. He thought that surely somewhere deep within there had to be some compassion, but she seldom, if ever, showed it. 'She was playing them for fools.', he knew now. 'This girl is to be watched.'

"It was not until I saw you all, saw this base and listened to the voices of your hearts that I knew you were no real threat to him or the people of this country.", she concluded.

"He sent you to kill us?", Bright Dusk inquired.

"Yes." She replied, flatly.

"These men are monsters. They will not hesitate to murder you in your sleep, send assassins to interrogate and even torture any of your family to get to you, mark me. You must not suffer them nor their messengers or mercenaries to live.", she added.

"But...to kill someone. I have never done such a thing." One of the younger bandits whimpered slightly.

Sen-hi leveled her eyes at him, "Hear me and know. War is not for the meek. It is a bold and bloody business. If you cannot dispatch your foe, you will never know victory."

"But I have seen Bright Dusk and the others leave some alive for questioning.", the bandit continued.

"The art of interrogation is vital for success in war, however, in a one-on-one fight, talk is worthless, less it is used to dishearten your opponent, steal their zeal for your own." The reality of her words hit home for some of the members of New Liberty.

"We may not all be as experienced in war as you, Sen-hi Sakeda, but we are eager to learn, knowing full well the risks and pitfalls in this endeavor. When we began this settlement, we were 100 in number, but with continued raids, coordinated attacks with ill enough time to recuperate and replenish, we have now lessened our population to a mere 25.", Bright Dusk said.

Sen-hi shook her head, "Nelson must have knowledge of the territories where your families live and you can be assured, since he sent me here, he would have surely sent others to them and..." She stopped, seeing the bristling terror in their eyes. Finally, she asked, "How many of you have been in actual combat?"

Only a few raised their hands, one of them being Bright Dusk himself.

"Most unfortunate. It would be best for you to think long and hard before continuing any further in this base of yours. Nelson and even Black are both accomplished and seasoned warriors.", she added.

"She's right, friends.", a voice from behind agreed.

Sen-hi turned when she heard the familiar voice. Her surprise was then coupled with shock and even some fear, for there, leaning against the threshold of the entrance of their hall was Captain Stephens.

Surprised beyond words, Sen-hi rose quickly, almost stumbling, facing the Captain as he simply stood there, seeming amused at her antics.

"I know not how or why you followed me here, Stephens, but I promise I will make you regret doing so...and in the process, fulfill the promise I made to you over your dinner table all those months ago."

In a flash, Sen-hi took to her sword, yet the blade would not answer to her call. It stuck to the sheath, unwilling, it appeared, to be used.

"It takes a great master of the ways of Sakeda to recognize an ambush before it happens, Sen-hi. It takes a god, however, to have the time to act upon it. Stay your blade, I am not come here for battle. I am here as an ally...and friend, if you will have me.", Stephens said plainly.

The party of bandits shifted as they watched in attention between the two potential combatants. "Explain to me, 'friend', why, not a month ago, I stood before you and General Nelson as he outlined my mission to locate and eliminate rebel factions of the military like this one. Explain how that mission was given in strict confidence to me whilst you were there and how you stand here before this assembly... still as a friend."

Stephens slowly unbelted his weapon, a Winchester Rifle, recently commissioned, and placed it calmly on the floor in between them.

"I have left the General's company, Sen-hi. He no longer speaks for this soldier's army and does not have the country's best interests at heart. The President..."

"How did his interests change since I last saw you both, since you were there taking the same orders as I?", she protested.

Captain Stephens sighed. "Sen-hi, I have never been in direct employ with General Nelson. I have always been a secret envoy and consult of President Grant. He has been suspicious of Nelson for some time now."

"And why did I not know of this, yet another wonderful secret, until now?", Sen-hi sighed.

"Not even you can know all things, Sen-hi. I never confided in anyone of my real allegiance. Not even my closest friends in my platoon knew. The only person that ever knew the truth was my most trusted servant and friend, Miss Anne."

Sen-hi smiled, "Well that is a true friend, then, for she never, not once, informed me of your treachery against Nelson. Keep that one close, Stephens. Far and few are ones like her."

"Oh, I be closer than butter on bread, girl!", with a gleeful skip in her pudgy step, Miss Anne bounded inside the main house, making a beeline for Sen-hi, who almost lost her balance, when the servant wrapped her in a tight bear hug. Holding her former student at arm's length, the jovial head house servant beamed, wiping away grit and greasy sweat off Sen-hi's face, revealing youthful lines.

"Oh, girl, I was worried sick o' you, I was. Cap'n Master here tol' me and tol' me you was safe, I ain't never been on a journey like this and oh, it was achin' me, so it was, girl! How are ya? Ya been eatin', not all but pig slop, I reckon. You sit tight, I cook ya up somethin' fair and tasty, fill up that belly of yours!"

With not but a word in edgewise, Miss Anne left the assembly house, looking feverishly for anything in any of the nearby houses resembling a kitchen.

"What can I say, I would be remiss leaving my best cook at home.", Stephens smiled and shrugged.

During the tense conversation, the leader, Bright Dusk, sat, hands folded under his chin in a ponder.

"I received intelligence someone would be sent here from the President's man, Captain, but did not know whom they would send.", he revealed.

"You knew of this as well?", she asked Captain Stephens. Sen-hi was shocked. How deep did this go?

"Yes, Sen-hi. Your involvement in this endeavor had been limited until now. You were only informed of Raven Black's evil plans. My connections to the Government were not made clear to you because, quite frankly, the President was not sure where your allegiance would end up. So, I will now ask. Now that you are aware of these things, who will you lend your impossible power to? Who will the heir of Sakeda side with?"

CHAPTER TEN

FABULIS ET CLAVES

The Presidio was a massive achievement of military construction and strategic placement. In its early history, the indigenous Ohlone and Costanoan people would seasonally occupy villages in what is now the San Francisco peninsula. From 1776 to 1821, the area was the Spanish empire's northernmost military outpost. That all changed when in 1846, during the Mexican-American War, the 7th New York Volunteer Infantry Regiment part of the settlements of the Presidio. The U.S. Regular Army then took over the post the following year. The General considered the history of this great fort and settlement as he was given the general tour by one of his Lieutenants. Behind them were four men wearing strange gas masks. The Lieutenant puzzled over their appearances. They had hoses coming out of their mouth filters and connecting to some kind of apparatus strapped to their backs. They looked like something out of a Jules Verne novel.

"The living quarters are further inside, Sir. Your house is in the centermost interior of the complex, nearest the barracks, where..."

"I need to be closer to the entrance, Lieutenant." The General seemed to be only half-listening as he continued, "If there's an attack, I want to be the first to know of it, not to be notified by courier or even trumpet blare."

"Yes, sir.", he responded.

General Nelson winced slightly as his mechanical arm's hinges pulled at the lip of skin they were connected to near his top shoulder muscles and tendons. With great care, he turned his back to the Lieutenant and pumped a primer located on the armpit of the mechanism and the metallic cables whirred and creaked, loosening their grip slightly.

"Have Captain Stephens...I mean Captain Davies and his officers put near the center." General Nelson's face contorted upon noticing his mistake of using his former Captain's name. He had been informed of Stephen's treachery, President Grant's missive that would have reached Stephens was intercepted by one of Nelson's loyal retainers and delivered to him personally. Severe measures would need to be taken. Nelson considered the many options and continued, "The Couriers' offices, as well as the horses and their trainers need to be better protected and have greater access to the compound's main entrance. If there's an attack by sea, I need those two towers up there manned with our biggest guns, our modified howitzers, you've been briefed, I take it?" The General asked, exposing his metallic arm slightly.

The Lieutenant bristled with some fear and nodded. "Good, let's get this ready, Lieutenant, I do not wish to lose another fortification to that Indian bastard and his redmen."

The two men walked on, the Lieutenant continuing to show the General the rest of the compound, however General Nelson was not the only one getting a tour. Unbeknownst to them, a small black eavesdropper was listening to everything the General said. The two men finally walked beyond sight, even beyond the Raven's sight, the Raven that was perched neatly on top of what was a nearby signpost. The Raven flapped its wings and flew away, landing on a horse almost a mile away from the fort. "What did you learn?", a voice from behind asked as the Raven cleaned his feathers and regarded the bush and rocks behind it.

"The fool has been well-informed. What of our base at El Catraz, that island the Spanish are so afraid of? It is closest to the fortress settlement, best to mount the invasion from there.", the Raven surmised.

"We have not taken the island yet, Master. We are just now preparing to take Fort Prospect.", the Mapiya Shadow Man said, emerging from the bush.

"Listen well, Brother Hanga, you will journey to the village stronghold near our Northern borders nearest Fort Prospect. Inform the men there they are to wait for my signal to begin the attack. I am to make a survey of the lands to the West. There is a disturbance there I must investigate."

"Master, I will never understand how you have made your body conform to the body of the Raven, though I will always be in awe of you."

"I prefer that you be in fear, Hanga. Be done with the job or I will make sport of you...for the crows. Or rather...Raven."

With a flick of his shiny wings, and a fiendish smile that should not belong on a bird, the Raven cawed with a mighty sound that seemed to fill the surrounding plain. Hanga looked on as the master of his tribe flew away. Fear had been his wish and fear, indeed, he would get.

The attack came without warning and from all sides. Sen-hi and her companion, Shaman Spirit Bear, were ambushed during their travels to find a way to defeat Raven Black, met with and assessed the very bandits that attacked them and now they fight again, except this time they fight with the ones that ambushed them against a large group of what look like Shadowmen right near the outskirts of their village, New Liberty.

"Try not to kill all of them, Sen-hi! We need some alive for answers!", the Shaman yelled.

Sen-hi only half-heard the Shaman from the other side of the encampment. She was far too busy fending off several attackers who decided to attack her at once. Nothing she wasn't used to, but she was in a strange land filled with different rules and spiritual power than she was accustomed to. These 'Shadowmen' fought unlike any man she had ever encountered. Their techniques were random, almost chaotic, in nature. They would swing their blades and weapons in what seemed like gravity-defying angles. Even their speed, agility and resilience to pain seemed inhuman. One of her opponents swiped what looked like a bo staff to her side, attempting to throw her off-balance, however, she saw this coming and side-stepped, making him stumble forward slightly instead. It was enough of a fumble to give her the opening she needed.

"Sakeda Ryu, Mantu Ryu Sen!", she uttered.

With blinding speed, her sword hit the ground and sent a tremor shaking around her, her quarry flying to all directions. Immediately, she pursued the one attacking her and, before he landed, launched another attack. "Sakeda Ryu, Choppu no Ken!". In one arc, her sword cut through the flying man like a hot knife through butter. The cut was so perfect and fast, the man's body didn't even bleed out until after landing on the ground. She did not have time to admire her work, though, because yet another attacker came upon her, this one with a Trident and Net.

"One would think I was fighting Ethiopians.", Sen-hi mumbled, blocking the Shadowman's Trident thrust with her sword's hilt just after sheathing it for battou-jutsu. Sen-hi's opponent was rather skilled with his weapon set. Usually, a Trident user relied on their weapon's weight in front for balance and used the polearm as a thrusting attack. With a quick jab, anyone with even mediocre strength could accomplish a well-executed impalement. This fighter knew this weapon and, instead, held the Trident closer to the fork end of the polearm. Sen-hi knew this to be an indication of her opponent's preference for offense and speed. It also meant he was not as experienced to defend. A quick dodge to the side afforded Sen-hi enough distance to space out her legs, one angled to her backside. With her sword already out, she switched her hold on the sword to a stabbing stance hold, the blade pointing straight out. Just as expected, the Shadowman lunged forward, right into the waiting maw of Sen-hi's mighty stabbing arc.

"Sakeda Ryu, Onara Ken Sen!" The air seemed to obey her every command. The stabbing motion she made with her sword brought forth a powerful gust of wind, and, instead of pushing the enemy backwards, it brought him forwards, straight into her blade!

Her enemy impaled and dispatched, she threw the corpse aside, waiting for her next battle. Instead, she found herself staring at a dust-filled landscape.

The warriors, Sen-hi and the Shaman performed marvelously. Still, even a great victory comes with its share of defeat, for one of the warriors had become gravely injured during the fray. The Shaman hastily instructed them to return to the tented village, where he could perform his healing magic on their colleague.

It had been almost two months since Sen-hi and Shaman Spirit Bear had made the camp with these outsiders their new home. Since then, they had come to learn a great deal about each of them, the story of how they came to be such a ragtag group, what their plans were and, ultimately, how she and her friend would fit in them. Despite it all, Sen-hi's tense relationship with Stephens had evolved into a slightly more friendly rivalry. There was more to this man that she did not know, did not have answers to. Why did he rescue her from that pit of hell of a prison and the traitorous Lieutenant Macarthur? Why did Stephens force her to learn English, treat her like one of his servants and to now begin treating her as one of his equals? Everything about him was contradictory. But more important things were afoot, so she put that out of her mind for now. The latest meeting had them discussing the latest information about Raven Black's activities with Captain Stephens.

"More and more, we see tribes joining Black and his Shadowmen. These men, however, were not fully initiated yet. The Shaman assures me he can turn them to help us, or at least provide us with information.", the Captain reported.

The group sat in their main meeting room, the smells of Miss Anne's dumpling stew emanating from the kitchen wafted through their hungry noses.

"It must be getting around that he's recruiting.", Bright Dusk remarked, marking the newest bases that the captured initiates let know about.

"The younger ones we captured during that last raid told the Shaman that a local 'leader of nations' is amassing an army to take on the U.S. Army.", Captain Stephens related, pointing to an unmarked and unexplored patch of the plains further North.

"They say there is a major Base Camp where this leader is set nice and pretty, north of Mount Shasta, the locals call it *Úytaahkoo*, whatever that means.", he concluded.

"It means 'white mountain' in the language of the Karuk tribe, Captain.", Shaman Spirit Bear interjected, continuing from where the Captain left off, "You will be certain to find many of Raven Black's encampments closer together and more heavily fortified the closer you get to that location."

"Do you think he will be there, Shaman?" Sen-hi asked.

"Doubtful. One of his higher ranking Warchiefs or Shaman-Chiefs will be in command of that base, I would think.", Spirit Bear responded.

"I thought you were his only Shaman?", Stephens asked.

"I was his most trusted friend and spiritual advisor, yes, Captain. But I am now branded a traitor and have most assuredly been replaced. Since he has brought a great many brother-tribes to his cause, you can expect such an answer to our paltry band of outcasts here the likes of which you have never seen.", Spirit Bear frowned.

"I have battled against forces of repute, Shaman, numbering in the thousands. Warriors of such skill, cunning and power that they would rival even Goki's forces.", Sen-hi leveled her gaze at the Shaman.

"I know not who this 'Goki' is, young warrior, but I assure you Raven Black is just as 'cunning' and powerful as any foe you have faced. Mark me! When I left his side, it was not because I disagreed with his politics. I left because I knew he had allied himself with darkness and that the path he was undertaking would bring all my brothers and sisters to a place they would never return. To hell, the Christians call it. So, if that fellow you mentioned ever had such a place as his headquarters, you can be assured Black will have just as dark and sinister a location. And worse still, I promise you."

Bright Dusk broke the tension by dropping a piece of paper on the table in between them.

"We just received word via wire from Washington of the supply source for the Shasta Base.", he relayed.

"What good does that do us? If we attack the source, they'll just set up another one somewhere else, and that's guessing they don't already have more bases for sources and supplies.", Lieutenant Steele added. Steele had become a valuable ally during the several months Sen-hi and Shaman Spirit Bear had joined New Liberty. His skill at intelligence gathering, as well as his prowess with the grapple-rope and technique with the rifle were rare indeed.

"Not if he doesn't know they were ever overtaken. And not if the main one is hit hard.", Bright Dusk proclaimed, pointing out the trail leading from the boon town of Dulces to the forest surrounding Mount Shasta.

"We can meet them during their supply run, here in the middle of where the high cliffs meet the plain, it takes a decline the closer it gets to the forest near Shasta. If we can take over that supply group, we can be assured entrance into the Base Camp at Shasta.", Steele said.

"How do you think they will allow you in, surely not by your looks." Sen-hi mused, eliciting a wink from Steele.

"Leave that to me, sugar." Steele countered, rolling up the map and taking his leave of the room.

"Steele and a group he chooses will engage the suppliers while another group awaits them inside the forest.", Stephens said.

"What would be their purpose?", Sen-hi asked.

"Do you see it, Sen-hi? The supply group would be…different at that point, savvy? They would enter the forest and from there, it will be a mad scramble to get to the entrance of that base."

"We do not know where the entrance is.", she pointed out.

"Correct, all we know is that it is hidden somewhere near the base of the Mountain, where it snakes through and ends up North of Shasta and inside the actual camp itself. There should be a trail there we can follow.", Bright Dusk said, searching the map.

"Damned thing could be anywhere in that forest." Stephens said, regarding his unshaven face.

"I trust you will find it or they will find you first.", Sen-hi said.

"That reminds me. Something one of them said made me think of you, Sen-hi." Stephens said. "They were talking about how one of them stumbled upon Black while he was engaged in some kind of dark ritual. I was hoping you or your Shaman friend could tell us more about it."

"Tell me.", Shaman Spirit Bear exchanged a suspicious glance with Sen-hi, doing his best to hide his slowly building anxiety. The small gathering listened as Stephens relayed the details of the witnessed ritual.

"A dark room, upside down triangle drawn on the sand with red-stained dust, outlined around it with a dark blue ellipse and a darkened stone in the dead center, glowing, pulsating with a darkened purple light. On each point of the triangle, a candle, halved and lit. Black himself in the center of the triangle, naked except for a cloth around his waist, and cradling the stone near the center of his chest. The initiate did not understand the words he was muttering to himself, just that the room would fill up with acrid smoke and shadows all around."

"And this glorious sight was beheld...without even a start from Black? Not likely.", Sen-hi snuffed her nose in the air, a clear sign of disbelief.

"Seems that way. He didn't make much sense after that, m'dear. Trailed off in ramblings after that, he indicated that the stone disappeared, it seemed. one of his higher ups kicked him out of the tent after that.", Stephens added plainly.

"Still, this changes nothing. Sounds like a normal meditat...", Sen-hi surmised.

"That was not a meditation ritual, Sen-hi." Spirit Bear interrupted, his face a mask of great concern. "If what you say is true, then it can only mean he was creating a contract in blood with the Raven himself."

"How can he create a contract with himself?", Sen-hi puzzled.

"Not the leader connecting with himself, young warrior, the contract is with the actual god Raven."

"That's enough for now, we can discuss all the riveting fantasy stuff another time, Shaman.", The Shaman looked at Bright Dusk with disappointment; This young tribal leader seemed disconnected somewhat from the spirits, that much was apparent. As his own village's Shaman, it saddened him to know whenever one of his brothers or sisters lost their way. He knew, though, learned, that Bright Dusk had many horrible experiences during his life on the run and during his time in the white eye military and it caused a spiritual rift within him. *Perhaps*, Spirit Bear thought, *this new experience will rekindle the flame of The Great Spirit within him and give him better medicine.*

"We must prepare for the task at hand.", Bright Dusk continued, pausing only a moment to take in the Shaman's saddened demeanor.

"Sen-hi, you, Stephens and Steele will head to Dulces to head the expedition into Shasta while myself and some of our group meet up with a few men from Stephens' old garrison. It still amazes me they weren't drummed out for abandoning Nelson, Captain.", Bright Dusk commanded.

"He isn't considered a part of the army anymore. President Grant has issued his removal at the earliest convenience.", Stephens emphasized.

"Well, that must wait until we capture this base, then." Bright Dusk affirmed.

"Wait!", the Shaman called out as the group was leaving the room. "There must be a change to this plan, Brother Bright Dusk."

The group's leader looked around in confusion, but motioned for him to continue.

"Sen-hi and I must have a quest of our own separate of this endeavor.", Spirit Bear said.

Bright Dusk rigidly refused, "I cannot afford to lose either of you. I'm sorry, no."

"Commander, listen! The ritual Captain Stephens described was no coincidence. Raven Black would never have allowed an intruder, regardless that it was one of his own men, anyone, to leave that tent alive, unless it was for an important reason.", Spirit Bear explained.

"He wanted us to know.", Sen-hi realized.

Shaman Spirit Bear nodded and continued, "Is it not odd that this group of invaders into our base were dispatched and captured so effortlessly? They were Shadowmen, uninitiated fully, yes, but still confirmed brethren to the Raven and his new 'ambassador', Raven Black."

"Didn't you convert them to our side, Shaman? Are you now saying we should kill them for traitors?", Bright Dusk asked.

"I merely removed the veil of shadow over their eyes, but their allegiance to Black will return in time, make no mistake. Take them with you on your journey, but do not kill them, they may be more valuable to you alive. Sen-hi and I must venture into the wilderness on our own important task."

"For what purpose?", Stephens demanded.

"If what the initiate said is true, if all these signs we have been witnessing are indeed coming to pass, we will need a greater ally and weapon than we already possess.", the Shaman regarded Sen-hi's sword with an almost ethereal gesture.

"You have always been a guest here, Shaman, therefore I cannot command you to stay, however, I must say I strongly disagree with this rash action. I am not an overtly spiritual man, I am sure you have already surmised that, however, I do not completely ignore Shamans' visions and teachings. I have found them to be somewhat helpful at times." Bright Dusk paused and nodded, "Very well, you are permitted to go your separate ways. I pray that whatever vision you are following is the right one. For all our sakes. I hope we meet again one day on the field of battle. Come, enough delay, we have preparations to make!"

Washington, D.C. - White House - President Grant's Cabinet Office

Senior Advisor to President Grant, Nathaniel Thomas was privy to many interesting conversations and goings-on as he meandered the maze of rooms that consisted of the overcrowded White House. After the War of 1812, the White House had to be rebuilt and even now it was almost impossible to find a room where a peaceful meeting could be held. Thomas chose the least uncomfortable end of one of the sofas in the common room, half-listening while two of President Grant's other advisors updated him on the mission given to a certain special 'Agent Stephens'. "We know he's made contact with the group, sir. The wire confirmed the leader to be none other than Bright Dusk, the...", the advisor said before being interrupted.

"The survivor of that massacre? That would make his cohorts easy to identify, then. Has he relayed our mission?", Grant asked, adding his signature to a document addressed to the Secretary of Treasury. "They discovered the location of what looks like one of Black's main armament camps, he is convinced it was the one you mentioned. I am sure they are already preparing the ambush of the supply train.", the advisor added.

"Did the girl make contact with the group yet? With the Indian Magic Man or...whatever they're called?"

"The Medicine Man, Shaman. Yes, sir."

"It seems, then, we're making some progress. What of our traitor, the General?", the President replied, a scowl crossing his face.

"He has taken hold of the Presidio, sir. We have not had word from there for too long.", Thomas replied.

"It would be unwise to attack it now, he would expect it and we do not know how many there are in league with him. Damn sloppy to let it fall.", President Grant blustered.

"He knows we are in a weak state, sir. We are still recovering from the War with the Confederates and still sending troops to populate our bases in the West.", Thomas said.

"Is it true these rumors I have heard? That he replaced his broken arm with...metal?", Grant twisted his mouth with what appeared to be disgust.

"We think so, sir. There was a Professor in residence at the Presidio who was a sort of genius in machinery. We think he is the one that built the arm. This is just rumors, sir. We have no idea if it is true."

"True or not, he is an idiot, throwing his career away, especially when we need him the most. I look forward to hearing the explanation for his treachery at his Court Martial. After the mission at the Mountain camp, have our group contact me. Also send word for our closest bases near the bay in San Francisco, nearest the Presidio, but not too close so as to reveal this intent; have them make ready for an assault at my command, but to do so without making any communiqués to other bases in the area. No supply runs, no new posts or commands. No one must make a move without a wire direct from this office.", Grant said flatly.

"Understood, Mr. President."

"And, one more thing."

"Sir?" President Grant looked over the cigar he had been enjoying, a slight frown of distaste molding his serious face. "Get me the name of our tobacco supplier. They're making these cigars too damned quick to stale."

CHAPTER ELEVEN
THE RAVEN'S EYES

The train of wagons, horses and men that consisted of the Karoba tribe carefully made their way towards the entrance of the Shadow Tribe's main camp. The perimeter of the Black's main headquarters, artfully and cleverly hidden deep within attacking distance from The Presidio, teemed with armed patrols of his most well-trained and seasoned Shadow Warriors. These men were fully turned and initiated into the dark world of the Shadow Stone, Black's newfound weapon against the white eye and the gods of light. They would not turn on him the way the others that had been sent to exterminate the Light's Champion had been. On horseback, they could easily patrol the outskirts of the base, reporting anything unusual to one of their adjutants within earshot. The patrollers' duty took them around the circular wall that surrounded the base and back towards the outside center, where was a massive gate, made up of two huge wooden doors controlled by more guards on the inside whose job it was to allow entry inside the compound. Watching over the gate and posted on opposing sides were watch towers, manned with lookouts, armed with a combination of bows and rifles. Raven Black's hut was located right in the center of the complex, a structure that resembled a chieftain's teepee, but with a stone foundation and two fire pits outside the entrance.

Inside, the Shadow Tribe Chieftain was in deep meditation,

the only light in the room was emanating from the shadow stone embedded deep in his chest, where his heart used to be. The visions he had were more infrequent now; he had to work extra hard to access the mind's eye and each time he did, there was a mist to overcome. With each attempt, the mist became thicker and harder to navigate through. Still, this time he found his destination: The beach. The very same beach where he discovered his destiny. And there on the shore, waiting for him, was The Raven himself.

"Kneel, adherent.", the entity commanded.

Raven Black flinched inwardly at the sound of the word coming from the dark bird-like entity. He never saw himself as anyone's servant and, even now with this new body and contract with the dark god, he felt the power of authority, not the other way around.

"I said kneel."

A wave of nausea overcame Black, a powerful, pressuring force that physically compelled him to kneel.

"That is as it should be. Now, you have all in place for the final assault, I take it?"

Black nodded and replied, "Yes, my lord. Macarthur's flight unit has been well-trained and await the order to attack."

"My other units...", Black emphasized the 'my', looking at The Raven for any sign of protest, but was answered with mere indifference.

Black scoffed, "...are also ready, all our bases have been alerted to empty immediately and head here. They have been instructed to arrive with great stealth."

"And have they all been trained to use the stone weapons properly?", it demanded.

"Yes."

The Raven peered into him, making the stone that was his heart pulse awkwardly, inducing another wave of nausea, which forced out of Black, "...my lord."

"Very well. I have more information on the Light's Champion. She will not be with the group headed to the Mountain base. This will give you an advantage in the final part of the plan. Did you acquire the obelisk?"

"My men are still searching for it...my lord.", Black hesitated again before saying it. Even knowing what the evil god would do to him if he didn't address him as lord, he would resist with every fiber of his being. Whatever being he had left, at any rate. The Raven grumbled at this news, sounding like a rumbling volcano about to erupt.

"The obelisk must be discovered before their Champion discovers it."

"Do not fret, my lord. My son and his best man were sent to retrieve it. Doubtful this girl would even know of the object, let alone where it is located."

"Fool!", the entity yelled in protest.

The ground around Black shook with the trembling power that came from The Raven's deep volcanic voice. If the tribal chieftain were covered head to toe in lava, he would not have been surprised.

"Always you court ignorance when you should guard yourself and that eye I gave you as a heart with great caution!", The Raven continued, "Do you not think this 'girl' cannot also commune with the light's forces the same way you commune with me? Think, Black! You have been given a great power and purpose. You must fulfill this and defeat her or everything we have worked for will be destroyed forever! Do you not wish to be rid of these white men and their kingdom of evil?"

"Yes, my lord!" For once, no hesitation.

"Do you want your land back?"

"Please, oh my lord Raven, please, yes!"

"Then you will do as I say, servant."

The word stung Black, but he fought back any attempt at rebuttal.

"Send two groups of bowmen and horse riders to guard the entrance to the harbor where your ships are docked. I sense an attack will come to you there soon. What of the General guarding The Presidio? How shall you deal with him?"

"He is merely a future corpse, that will be destroyed in the first wave. Why should I treat him any differently?"

"Do not underestimate him, Black. You have a place of advantage that you should not take lightly. His superiors are not pleased with him. If you time this attack correctly, you will have an unexpected ally against the Americans' army. I would exercise caution on when you implement this strategy.", the entity leveled its pitch black eyes into his soul.

"I have everything in control, my lord. As soon as our last remaining forces are in place, which should be very soon, I will attack with my full force.", Black attempted to sound as confident as possible, but how successful could that be against such a force?

The Raven stood there, judging Black and his words with great suspicion. With a wave of his massive wings, Black's vision was broken and he was thrust back into the world.

Just then, one of his guards barked from the outside, "Lord Black, a messenger from our sister tribe has arrived. The Karoba are here."

With a grin, Black arose and exited his tent. "Excellent. Assemble the tribal leaders for a drum circle outside this tent. The time has arrived."

The Shaman and Sen-hi were well underway on the quest Shaman Spirit Bear mentioned. Each time Sen-hi asked him, The Shaman would only mention that it was 'important' they go on this quest and that the item they were retrieving would be extremely valuable for the coming struggle with the Shadow Tribe. They would travel for days on horseback, stopping only to water and feed the horses, trotting beside them to offer respite. Timing was essential, because the Shaman insisted they sleep on the saddle. After almost two weeks of travel, they arrived at the banks of a large river as night had just descended. The two companions had gotten to know each other very well over these past months. Sen-hi had missed the camaraderie and debate of being around her Samurai brethren in Japan, but being with this mysticist, as she viewed him, was a truly unique experience. Shaman Spirit Bear was a very open-minded man, worldly in his knowledge and breadth of experience, his thoughts on most topics like tribal unity and the mass colonization of the white men ranged from slightly optimistic to extremely cautious.

"Has being in our land all this time given you any pause to its beauty?", the Shaman asked as a star flew through the night sky.

Sen-hi poked a stick into their slowly growing fire and proceeded to clean her beloved sword.

"We have rivers and skies in my homeland as well, Shaman.", she pointed out.

"I am aware of that, young one. Do you not have any regard for..."

"I am a Samurai. We are a proud race of warriors and do not have time for...regard.", she smirked, looking down the blade of her sword for any blemishes.

"How very sad." The pain on his face was evident as he looked at her carefully tending to her sword. An instrument of murder and death, he fretted.

"You know, to a person whose entire life is killing, the world must indeed seem a very dull and lifeless place."

"Sakeda Ryu, Dakei No Ken."

With a quick strike, her sword hit the ground with tremendous force, sending up a shower of sparks and rocks. The Shaman reeled from the shock of seeing his young companion perform such a violent maneuver so close to him and looked at her, more in shock than in fear.

"The ground is just as beautiful stark and naked as it is damaged and bloody. What purpose have we travelled this distance for?", her voice rumbled with purpose, sending shivers down Spirit Bear's spine. Still, he would not relent.

"Sen-hi, do you never wish to discuss anything un-related to warfare or fighting General Nelson or Raven Black?", he sighed, poking the fire.

"No outside forces, Shaman.", she simply stated.

Shaman Spirit Bear's confused demeanor pressed her to explain.

"The most important mantra of my sword's law is that a Samurai must never permit any outside forces to infiltrate and influence their path of sword."

"But that can mean anything! Do you mean to say that you Samurai can never think of anything but battle? You can never ponder on the marvels of a sunrise or sunset? The majesty of a butterfly as it emerges from its cocoon or how the rain dances upon the meadow just as it dances upon the backs of the travelling bison? Can you love, Sen-hi Sakeda?"

Sen-hi's eyes glistened for a moment, but the Shaman could not tell whether it was a flicker of emotion or the reflection of the moonlight. Slowly, she undid her obi tie, without completely undressing her hakama and lifted her upper jacket without exposing her breasts. Instinctively, the Shaman averted his gaze, but she redirected him.

"If you can look for a moment, you will see the consequences of allowing 'love' to interfere with my Bushido."

He had seen many scars and wounds in his life as a Shaman, however, the damage he was seeing now was something entirely different. She had a long deep scar from just above her waist until just below her right breast. He could tell it had been there for a time and that it would have killed her if it had been any lower.

"The person who did this...how did...I mean, I thought you were invincible?", he wondered.

"So did I and that is yet another reason why I must never allow any outside forces to invade my way of the sword. Or my being."

As she tucked her jacket back in, for just a moment, he could see a young child struggling to comprehend a greater world that existed outside her own, yet also trying to let her into it. He pitied her, he realized, for not knowing the love of Mother Earth, of The Great Spirit, and wondered if anything or anyone could ever bring that forth in her.

Looking towards the Crescent Moon, he smiled slightly and thought to himself, "In the morning, I will have my answer."

Shaman Spirit Bear awoke to the sounds of nature, reveling in all the wonders around him as he prepared for the journey ahead. In the distance, he could see his companion undergoing some kind of physical exercise.

After breakfast and letting down of their camp site, he asked, "What were you doing over there?"

"Chinkon Kishin. It is an ancient technique used to calm the spirit and return it to its source. Not all Samurai practice it, however, one of my instructors in my village of Ikeda-haji was a Shinto monk who taught me a great many things.", she said completing the exercise as they mounted their horses.

The Shaman smiled and directed their horses ahead to what looked like a cliff. "Then let me show you a return to a different source of spirit...and our destination." Ahead of them, Sen-hi paused and actually marveled at the majestic sight in front of them: the biggest crevice she had ever seen. Extending for what seemed like miles in either direction, the cliff had many ways down and no way across. As she looked into the massive canyon, she could see some trails that were man-made and others that the Earth had made from ancient floods or earthquakes. Ahead was the other side of the canyon, another cliff face with more trails and caves.

"What...is this place?", Sen-hi asked, almost at a loss for words.

"The white man calls it The Grand Canyon, however, the local Hopi call her Ongtupqa and the Wi:ka'i:la people call her Yavapai. She is the mother of this land we have come to and houses the one we must see, The Sasquatch Skinwalker."

Along the edges of the Sacramento River, the group comprised of Captain Stephens and ten Marines sent to rendezvous with him waited, along with Brittany and Hector Sanchez, twin Mestizos that were taken in by Bright Dusk and the New Liberty members, Chen Xie, a Chinese acrobat that recently came into their village's membership and Lieutenant Chris Steele.

The sun had just begun to set when Captain Stephens motioned for the party to stop and camp near a large overturned stone face near the river.

"This will give us some cover for the night. Make sure to make the fire small and direct the smoke towards the river. Lieutenant, you and the Marine platoon are to make two patrol points, both at the lip of the river near us and a smaller patrol no more than one horse stop behind us. Make their routes as narrow as possible and position lookouts high up on the trees. Report any anomalies."

With a snappy salute, Steele left the camp as the New Liberty recruits set up the camp. Brittany and Hector shared a good natured laugh at the expense of the Captain as he tripped over a fallen branch he did not see and he tossed it at their feet.

"Since you think that's so funny, why don't you two jokers toss that in the fire."

"What fire? There's no fire?", Brittany noted, looking around the camp.

"There will be when you make one.", Stephens stated.

With a smug look, she and her brother gathered some kindling together and prepared the fire. Great care was taken to make sure the smoke would not billow too much, however, no matter how much they tried, they could not get the fire to lessen in intensity. The Chinese New Liberty member saw this and instructed, "Do they not teach you Westerners how to make proper fires when you are trying to conceal your location? Dig a fire pit first, place small rocks on the bottom, small dry wood. We also need to be sure we place it inside this rock face so whatever smoke escapes, comes out dissipates quickly."

"Well aren't you helpful!"

"Yeah, if he's so helpful, why can't he cook me a decent steak, sis?!" Brittany and Hector giggled, setting up the remainder of their campsite as Stephens laid out a map.

Further across the river, the Marine compliment assigned to Stephens' group distribute the rations and go over their plan of attack as the senior officer for the group, Colonel Beiro, arranged a small layout on an flat, slightly angular rock outcrop that looks like a smaller version of the area they are in, including where they believe the Shasta camp is.

"When the word is given, we will spread out in the pre-arranged groups and head towards this point where the wagon train is supposed to stop for camp before making their last turn towards the base. Sergeant Hanusi, you and your group will be the ones taking the flank once we see the wagon train from a distance. Remember, our timing is everything. Once they see us, they will attempt to send scouts to warn their base that we are here. Hanusi, you and your group are to locate and stop those scouts." Hanusi nodded in agreement and Beiro dismissed the group to their posts for the night.

Later that night, one of the high and hide lookouts in the trees, Private Angelo Lowrie, a new recruit to the New Liberty group assigned to Stephens' infantry unit, almost nodded off when he noticed something in the distance. It looked like part of the forest itself was moving. The tree line was swaying in random, sometimes sharp motions against the direction of the wind, but that is impossible. Unless something was moving on the ground near the commotion. Before giving the agreed upon alarm signal, he took out his telescope and focused down into the moving foliage. Blurry green and brown leaves and branches filled his eyepiece until, finally, he saw the telltale muslin tarp cover and the three ringed shapes bending up so as to stand up the cover. The wagon train had arrived. Immediately, Lowrie took out his duck call and, just as be put it to his lips, a sheer high whistling sound made its way through the tree tops and silenced Private Lowrie with an arrow shaft right through his windpipe. His cry of death could not be heard as he drowned in his own blood, slumped against the thick pine's trunk.

Down in their campsite, Captain Stephens finished his sumptuous meal of beans and pig fat. Never being one to tolerate a mess, he fastidiously cleaned his 'plate', really a small tin cup he used both as something to eat out of and to make coffee in. He remembered the first time he was given it by his one-time friend, General Nelson.

'Can't believe this is happening, Thomas.', Stephens mentally struggled against the reality he was engulfed in. He had known Thomas Nelson since the two attended WestPoint together. They had been through life and death during the Civil War and it was during that time, in the battle of Gettysburg itself, that changed Nelson forever. Hell, there wasn't a man that survived that massacre that hadn't changed, Stephens scoffed.

Still, nothing that had transpired over the years could have lead him to understand or believe that his friend, now his enemy, was this different. Why the metallic arm? And why make such a dramatic show of force against the military? It was beyond irregular, damn it all. To say nothing, Stephens mused, about this Japanese girl that stumbled onto his life.

"Copy Samurai", Stephens laughed a little in spite of himself as he stirred the boiling water into the coffee grounds.

"I'm no damn Samurai, just a real good study." He yelped slightly as the hot coffee stung his throat and allowed himself another small laugh. And it was indeed short lived, for in a blink of an eye, the camp was alive with frantic activity.

Stephens doused the fire in a rush and called out the nearest soldier, "What's the problem? You'll give away our position, damn it!"

"Too late for that, Captain!", Private Hector yelled, swinging his rifle around his shoulder, "The wagon train, they know we're here, sent out a compliment of sharpshooters and bowmen to our camp across the river already. We're gettin' our gear together to fight back!"

Stephens snapped his jacket closed and grabbed his rifle, bullet pouch and sword. "To battle, then! Take me to the front lines, soldier!"

CHAPTER TWELVE
THE SKINWALKER

Down into the ravine, Sen-hi and Shaman Spirit Bear trotted their horses, carefully plotting each step, making sure not to disturb anything that looked remotely dangerous on the trail. The old rock face of The Grand Canyon had just been converted to a trail for interested visitors to walk on, however, it was not complete and there were still many places where a traveler could lose their footing and their life.

Sen-hi adjusted the obi on her hakama to compensate for the rugged terrain and wiped a line of sweat from her brow. Just above, an eagle soared overhead. As practiced as ever, without saying a word to the Shaman, she flipped open her eyepatch and reached out for the great bird with her power. Just as she had hoped, it became much easier with each try and she was already seeing herself and her companion from way above the canyon's crevice and cliff wall. She, now the eagle, took note that her human body stood still, understandably, looking up. With a great flap of her wings, feeling the warm gust of air from the canyon below, she dove down and landed firmly upon her own shoulder. As a bird, she could feel the sting of her own talons on her right wing as she dug in. "Young one, that was impressive, but we have arrived.", Spirit Bear pointed out.

With a simple command, she disconnected from the Eagle and it now stared at her with great respect and silence. Sen-hi was shocked that it would not claw at her, but she also knew it never would, she, after all, now knew everything about this beautiful animal, just by being it for a brief moment. The Eagle seemed to bow to her for a moment and flew off. "You must feed them, Mother, I know. Where is this Skinwalker, Shaman?", she asked, admiring the eagle as it flew away.

The Shaman pointed to a large opening on the side of the cliff floor below, within a rocky outcropping. The two made their way to the cave and the Shaman motioned for silence as he peered inside.

"He is not inside. He must be out hunting. We are to wait here until he returns."

Sen-hi positioned herself a short distance from the cave's entrance, her hand strategically placed on her sword. The Shaman proceeded to untie a rabbit that he had caught and killed earlier that day and placed it near the cave.

When Sen-hi looked at him doing this, he smiled and responded, "An offering of peace, young one. Or he is as like to eat us as this rabbit."

With a haughty turn of her eyes, Sen-hi took in her surroundings carefully, making sure to look within any cracks or shadows for movement of any type. Suddenly, a large shape made its presence known coming out of another cave across them. Sen-hi tensed her sword's grip as she saw a great black bear emerge and walk towards them. The Shaman eased his hands in front of Sen-hi, urging her to calm herself. Slowly, he walked away from the cave, Sen-hi following but not taking her eyes away from the beast. The hairy monstrosity pawed its way to the cave entrance they had just been at and stopped short of the Shaman's 'offering'.

With a grunt and great scoffing exhale, the bear turned to them both and let out a gut-churning bellow, the likes of which Sen-hi had never seen before.

"Be at peace, Sasquatch. I am Spirit Bear, Man of Medicine and Shaman of the once proud tribe of Mapiya. I come to you under grave circumstances seeking your power and help to defeat the evil of the raven and his minions of evil.", Spirit Bear said, a peaceful tone emanating from each word.

The bear did not seem to listen or care, for it proceeded to thud down the side of the rocks, closer to the duo. Sen-hi peered at the animal and looked confusingly at The Shaman.

"Are you sure this is what we're waiting for?", she said, watching the animal closely.

The Shaman wiped cold sweat from his forehead and shrugged, "Yes. No. I am not sure. Prepare to defend yourself, but do not kill him. It sometimes takes a moment for him to remember that he is human."

Sen-hi gave a resigned sigh and undid her sword belt, using it as a headband. She leveled her gaze at the bear and said, "I know not whether you understand me, Skinwalker, but I do not have the time to wait for you. Our friends' lives are in danger and I need your help to defeat Raven black and his Shadow Tribe. Will you help us or will you feel the tip of the sword of Sakeda?"

With a roar that seemed to shake the walls of the canyon itself, the bear rose to its full height and threatened Sen-hi with a raised claw. In a tremendous show of force, the paw came down upon Sen-hi, who just barely dodged out of the way. She looked on in stunning awe as its paw smashed a large rock she was standing on.

"So be it. Sakeda Ryu, Menosameruyou No Ken!" With a side swipe of her sheath, she reached out to strike the bear, only to hit its extended arm with a dull thud. The bear showed no sign of pain and instead responded by batting her sword back at her with a roar of defiance. In short succession, it charged at her and chomped down at her arm, catching, with great luck for her, the lip of her sleeve. The bear wiped away the cloth with its paw and charged again, teeth bared and maw gaping wide. Sen-hi spit in frustration, positioning herself for another attack.

"Sen-hi, do not antagonize him! Defend yourself only!"

"Silence, Shaman! I will not be killed by a dumb animal! Sakeda Ryu, Ken No..."

The bear, with the speed of lightning, crashed on top of her in a great heap, the sound of crunching bone and rock filling the ground around her. Shaman Spirit Bear instinctively took out his medicine pouch and emptied its contents upon the ground. He then began chanting in Mapiyan.

No matter what Sen-hi could do, she was utterly powerless beneath this monstrous animal. As the animal's foul breath filled her lungs and dripping bear saliva followed her cheek line, she felt real fear. She then did the only thing she could think of: She opened her eye patch and reached...and what she found was even more horrifying than she could imagine.

At the end of the void and abyss, instead of her own face looking back at her own, she saw two eyes. Eyes that were filled with hatred and anger. Eyes filled with the promise of death. She wished just then that she had never attempted to take possession of this animal. She now knew this was, indeed, no animal. This was a man and he was angry.

"Do you wish to control me, girl?" The raspy, thunderous voice filled her head in the void. "Do you think you have the ability? Perhaps I should show you what real control is.", the man said with a growl.

In a violent thrust, Sen-hi felt herself pushed out of the void and into her own body, however, she realized in horror she was no longer in control of it! Still hearing the other voice, she struggled against it, against him. "Yes, do try to fight me, young warrior. Fight me, because I intend to make you regret ever disrespecting me.", he said, sneering.

In abject terror, she looked on as the bear that was almost above her before walked back slowly and then rose to its full height, opening its mouth wide, blood dripping from its long fangs.

"That blood is not mine, woman.", he said.

She felt her head turn against her will and look at her shoulder, which had two puncture wounds.

"You dare to come into here, you dare to show me such disrespect with such a weak offering? You do not belong here!", the bear roared, bounding upon her. With the strength of spirit that she only hoped she had, Sen-hi screamed inside her head, primal fear and instinctual power fuming from her every pore, against this unseen foe. Suddenly, the animal paused in its gait, with a strange look in its eyes. At this moment, Sen-hi broke free of the hold he had upon her and went for her sword.

"You will now feel the blade of justice, beast!" But the sword would not answer her. She struggled and pulled, but the sword remained sheathed.

"Remember, young one, it may only be used as a sword of justice. You will not need it, I have reached him, finally.", the Shaman said.

Sen-hi turned as the Shaman approached their position. Sen-hi then looked on in muted awe as the bear changed in front of them. Slowly, the hair receded across its chest, arms and legs. The paws shrunk to become...hands, Sen-hi thought? The fangs retracted, sweat and saliva covering the transforming body. Where a bear had been, a man now stood. But for all his humanity, the eyes, those same anger-filled bear-like eyes, stayed the same.

"Come, Sasquatch, we have much to discuss and time is precious and fleeting.", Spirit Bear pleaded.

With reluctance, the naked man led them to the cave. Before entering, he picked up the rabbit, tore off its head and began eating it as they entered his home.

The huge rocks outside acted as a natural cover for the real entrance of the cave, where the foot of one large cliff face ended flat and curved towards the inside of the mountain itself. Erosion did the rest and offered a rather large living space for the Skinwalker. The interior wall was peppered with an assortment of animal skins, stretched and tanned as if by a master leatherworker. A quiver and arrow set lay against a hay-filled mat and un-used fire pit against the back wall and some long, flat rocks that acted as a stony frame for his bedding.

The companions were pointed to sit as the Skinwalker skinned the rabbit and prepared it for a meal. He then paused and lit a flame, a look brushed across his face that was something between guilt and self-awareness. "I am not accustomed to visitors.", he uttered, offering them some tobacco. Sen-hi had never gotten used to the leafy drug that the natives enjoyed. She politely declined to smoke it, but pocketed it anyway, knowing it would be disrespectful to deny it completely.

"We come to speak of the magic stones that our people had found within the mountains, Sasquatch. They have strange properties that...", Spirit Bear paused, looking to Sasquatch.

The Skinwalker raised a hand slightly covered with what looked like a cross between human and animal hair and interrupted, "I know all about the stones, Brother Mapiya. Did one of your tribe brothers or sisters ingest the stone or use it as a fire stick?"

"No, my Elder and Brother, once-called Proud Eagle, used it in a dark ritual to commune and merge with the Raven itself. He is now called Raven Black.", he explained.

"He is no longer human, then, if that is his new name. It seems I require a great deal of information and you do not have the time to explain it to me. Are you familiar with the ritual of vision of mind?"

"Yes, that would be agreeable. We would need to acquire the necessary herbs.", Spirit Bear nodded.

"No need, I already have them. I take Vision Quests often in my quest to find the perfect animal path."

The Skinwalker produced a pouch from a makeshift shelf behind him and emptied the contents into the dry fire pit in between him and the Shaman. With a snap of a few stones, the fire breathed life and produced a bright blue light. Sasquatch then inhaled into a long wooden pipe and allowed the fumes to remain inside of him. He then gave the pipe to the Shaman, who did the same thing. Almost immediately thereafter, both the Shaman and Sasquatch stared intently into each other's eyes and the blue light blazed high. Sen-hi was taken aback by this ceremony and wondered what purpose it could possibly have. All of the rituals she had witnessed from this 'man of medicine' had been fantastical in nature. From the smoking of his pipes to the rhythmic dancing and chanting around large bonfires during their long treks across the wilderness.

After what seemed like hours, the blue light dissipated to a small orange-red flame and the two men nodded to each other.

"I see your thoughts, brother.", the Skinwalker revealed, breathing deeply as he placed his closed outstretched right hand over his forehead and then over his heart. "Your enemy is a truly powerful one and must be destroyed for all of our sakes, else the white eye will use this as a catalyst to exterminate all of us."

"Precisely, brother. The fact that my old friend has become this monster troubles me greater than anything else. Is there a way to reach him and stop this madness?", Spirit Bear added.

Sasquatch paused and looked at the Shaman with great sadness.

"No, I am very sorry. He is no longer human. The fact that he cooperated in the dark ritual of Enigonhahetgea signifies that he has sided with the dark one. He is now the raven's avatar.", he said, flatly.

"What do you mean, 'avatar'?" Sen-hi asked, getting an annoyed reaction from Sasquatch.

"There are two gods in this land, young warrior: Both are known as The Raven, but both are separate. One Raven is the god of darkness and chaos, father of lies and misfortune, while the other Raven is the god of light and goodness, father of power.", Sasquatch said, pausing to stretch his very hairy legs.

"These two gods are actually sons of the Mother of creation, Skywoman, who is also called The Great Spirit. Some of our brothers see her as a he, but the Great Spirit is a woman, I guarantee it. She originally lived on a floating island above a great ocean. While there, she gave birth to twins, the good and bad raven gods. The bad raven twin was born first and brought into the world darkness and despair. This made Sky Woman sad and, in her sadness, begat good raven, who saw his mother's sadness and brought light and happiness into the world. This made bad twin brother raven enraged and the twins became entwined into an epic battle between good and evil. During their tumult, the earth shook and the seas trembled and exploded. Finally, the good raven god expelled his dark twin into the nether world of evil spirits and light was forever a part of the world. But their fight caused the island that the Sky Woman had lived on to break apart and she began falling. She was weak, therefore, and the few animals that had survived the cataclysm in the ocean took pity on her and formed mud out of their saliva and sand from under the water for her to stand on. So did she land upon this firmament and began creating mountains, forests, rivers and great plains filled with all manner of beasts. This is how our land was created."

"But you said the dark god was expelled. How, if what you say is true, did he escape and pollute the mind of this tribal leader?", Sen-hi posed.

"A good question. I can only assume that he was permitted to enter into our world through the veil of strife, brought upon us all by..."

"Dear Buddha, yes, by the fighting between the Americans and your people.", Sen-hi inserted.

The Skinwalker simply nodded in affirmation.

"So, if he is a god, how do we defeat him?", she asked in desperation.

"Not easily, to be sure, but it can be done and must be done quickly. As it stands now, Raven Black is merely an avatar for the dark god, this means there is a part of him that is still human and, thus, can be harmed. The stone he used to complete the communion ritual with the dark one is the key. You must break the stone in order to sever the link between him and the Raven. If you do this, he will become human for a period of time and it is during that time you must render him inert."

"I'll do more than that. I'll render him dead!", Sen-hi declared with confidence.

The Shaman waved in disagreement, "No, my child. You must not kill him. That is not the way."

"What? But you just heard your friend. This man has already made a dark pact with an evil god, if we allow him to live, who knows what greater evil he will perpetrate in the future?"

"Sen-hi, he made that pact because the white eye...", Spirit Bear attempted to clarify.

"It does not matter the reason behind his actions, Shaman. No reason should ever bring a man to make deals with devils. I am aware of your friendship with him, but you must also realize that died the moment he became one with the stone. I must defeat him totally. For the sake of all that is good and decent in this world.", she explained.

The Skinwalker's pained eyes glazed over with animalistic intensity as he said, "Sen-hi, daughter of the blade of Sakeda, do you feel yourself to be the only 'avatar' of justice for this world? Do not put upon yourself the burdens of judgment for the whole of mankind. Justice is a concept best left for the gods, young one."

"The gods do not own this planet. Skinwalker, man does. I will not stand idly by while my friends risk their lives against this madman. Your words are truly beautiful and filled with wisdom, great Sasquatch, however, I am not a native of this land. I am Japanese and must remain Japanese in my methods."

Seeing that she was resigned in her actions, the two men exchanged a concerned, but ultimately hopeful look.

"Perhaps The Great Spirit has a unique path for you to follow. More importantly, you will not be able to penetrate Raven Black's skin with that sword."

Sen-hi scoffed, "You have no idea how powerful this sword is.", she said, admiring her sword as she held it in display for the two men.

"It is not in the power of the blade that I speak of, it is in its intent. Earlier, you could not unsheathe your sword to strike me, correct? Your sword is to be used as a tool for justice, not vengeance or outright bloodshed. In order to hurt your enemy, you must use a different weapon. A natural one.", he said standing up.

Behind one of the tanning stands, Sasquatch pulled out a long wooden box. The box itself looked as if it was carved out of an old tree branch. It had etchings all over it and even the hinges looked wooden, or at least, the metal was rusted to the point that it matched the color of the surrounding wood.

"This is a truly sacred object for our people, the ones that are of the Mountains. I am the last of their kind and was entrusted this by my tribal elder. Its natural state is that of a bow and empty quiver, which fills of its own accord with arrows made of the hardest oak and heads of blackest obsidian. It is the Bow of Adistan, for it listens to your spirit.", he said giving the objects to her. As he handed the bow and quiver to Sen-hi, a powerful energy surged through her and, at once, she understood the power behind the bow.

"I can change it." She breathed, handling the bow and, with a flap of her eye patch, she reached into the weapon. In her mind's eye, she saw a bo staff and, as she formed it and opened herself back into the world, she marveled as the bow had indeed become a Bo Staff!

"What a marvelous gift! Sasquatch, are you certain this is acceptable for us...for her?", Spirit Bear's excitement was evident.

Sasquatch nodded his approval and pointed above them. "It is the will of The Great Spirit that you have found me, brother...yes, and sister of another shore. No one ever finds me twice and those that find me once are said to not recall ever finding me at all. Go from this place and use this relic as you deem fit, for it is now yours, Sen-hi. My time as a man grows thin and you do not wish to be here much longer.", he stated, a glint of energy growing slightly larger in his eyes.

They did not need to hear any more. They made their way out of the cave and were amazed as they noticed the same cave they had just exited turning into a flattened, rocky wall. The Sasquatch was gone, as was any sign of Sen-hi's struggle with him.

"Your wound is healed!", the Shaman noted with great relief. Truly, her sleeve was no longer bloody and her hakama sleeve was mended as if it had never been torn. But she still had the Bow of Aditsan.

"Come, Shaman, we must...", she was about to say when, with a sudden blast of rock and dust, Sen-hi and her companion were thrown like rag dolls against the mountainside.

Sen-hi's warrior instincts kicked in and she jumped to her feet, her sword immediately unsheathed and ready for battle. To her side, she could see the Shaman's body moving, alive. Ahead of them was a long, black metallic cable stretched to the ground, where it stuck hard, held in place with what looked like a big anchor. She followed the cable up and was astounded when she saw what it was connected to: A massive floating airship. The behemoth was floating high above them, a balloon-like vehicle, the balloon itself shaped like a sort of cigar, tethered with cables similar to the one attached to the anchor, to what looked like a great canoe, but much wider in order to carry more men and supplies, Sen-hi surmised. The balloon section itself was covered with what looked like a massive leather skin, painted dark but with tribal war paint, kinked in three different places by something poking from underneath. Sen-hi could only assume those three indentations had to be strong, metallic perhaps. But she had little time after that to make anymore observations, for the men that were inside that canoe-like boat were descending down into the canyon using the cable and anchor as a directing target.

"Defend yourself, Shaman! We have an ambush!" The Shaman took out his tomahawk and began swiping at the two nearest Shadowmen, both brandishing those telltale sabers.

"Our master told us you would be here, foreign woman. You will fall here as your friends will fall near Mount Úytaahkoo!", one of the Shadowmen yelled.

Sen-hi sneered and positioned herself quickly, "Sakeda Ryu, Mantu Ryu Sen!" With a tap of her hilt on the ground, Sen-hi jumped backwards, her blade swishing across the air in front of her and, unbelievably, to her sides, causing five of her assailants to reel back with heavy slash wounds across their chests.

"You are sadly mistaken if you believe yourselves to be the harbingers of my doom, men of Shadow. Sakeda Ryu, Kaze No Ryoukan!" Where her blade had ended, outstretched to her side, she turned it and unleashed it again the opposite way, causing a powerful gust of wind to emanate from the swinging arc. The gust was so powerful, that it blasted the same five men on their backs. As they lay there, she could see a faint black glow within each of their palms. 'The stone'.

With a final stance of her sword sheathed, Sen-hi uttered, "Sakeda Ryu, Kushi No Ken!" as she unsheathed and impaled them with lightning speed, all by their palms, in perfect aim with the glow. Claiming victory, Sen-hi unceremoniously swiped her sword to the side, the blackened blood sizzling as it was thrown against the stone face of the mountain. Slowly it turned red, free of taint, she realized. With contempt for the black magic, she looked at the Shadow soldiers, lying still on the floor, gripping their now useless hands and crying in pain. She also saw that their armor and purple coloring of their skin was slowly dissipating.

"Your god seems to desert you after I make his connection to you forfeit. Shall I end your misery, fools?", she asked, raising her sword, the light of the sun glinting on its pristine surface.

"By all that is holy, have mercy! We were only following orders!", one of them pleaded, holding both hands, even the bloody one, in front of him in desperate prayer to Sen-hi.

"Give me information and I might let you live. What is the purpose of this dirigible? Are there others and, if so, where will your Master, Raven Black, strike?", she commanded.

One of the soldiers mewled in fear and responded, "Yes, yes, all right, just please do not kill us! He spoke of attacking a great fortress of the Army, located along the shore of an ocean with a mighty span to another shore, connected by a golden gate of water. We were sent here to kill you while the group near our camp in the shadow of the Mountain would be ambushed and used as hostages for the final battle. I swear that is all we were told!"

Sen-hi slowly sheathed her sword and turned her back on them. The Shadowmen, now completely devoid of the Shadow's power, breathed a sigh of relief as Sen-hi threw down a loop of rope in front of them. Seeing their bleeding hands still, she tossed them a bundle of linen and ointment.

"Clean yourselves up. You're coming with us."

"You have broken the Shadow's grip from us. We are your humble servants, now, Lady of a Thousand Blades! Where are we going?"

"To change the destiny of your people."

CHAPTER THIRTEEN
GOLDEN DAWN

Private Matthias was relieved to end his patrol across the great walls encircling the great Army headquarters known as The Presidio. He had promised himself a ride on the ferry to go hiking when the day was done, but this would not be permitted today. The Presidio was on lockdown after General Nelson issued a general announcement of an imminent threat of attack. Matthias laughed at the thought. An attack on one of the nation's most defensible structures. The fortress was, after all, known far and wide for its strategic placement upon the harbors and shores of San Francisco Bay, connected to the other side of the bay by The Golden Gate of San Francisco, an immense span of ocean separating The Presidio and the rest of San Francisco from Marin County to the North. The port on the San Francisco side was a very popular port for trade, used by the Sausalito Land and Ferry Company to transport water, trade goods and human passengers across the bay. The ferry service had been so popular, in fact, that some automobiles, brand new mechanical marvels of transportation that moved on four wheels using newfound gasoline as its fuel instead of horses, could be seen on rare occasions on the transports. The General, however, issued an order to discontinue the use of the Ferry until the threat had passed. This left hundreds, perhaps close to a thousand, passengers marooned on both sides of the bay, most of them inside the base. All civilian family members were ordered to remain inside the civilian quarters, newly built two-story haciendas on the far eastern side of the fortress. Nelson was a master strategist, employing the use of the Gatling guns along the upper parts of the wall, using the cannons as a defensive measure at key points on the outer wall itself. Separate groups of soldiers were placed on patrolling runs, Matthias being one of them. They were to call out any unusual activity or sign of intrusion along the path leading to the base from the Mountains to the South or the ocean along the North, West and East. Nestled in a Command Tent, Nelson looked over schematics and design maps for the base. He also toiled over several reports of enemy activity, wires from posts that were still loyal to him, as well as others that had not heard of his dissent from the U.S. Military. His officers closest to him that had still remained after the defection stood around the table, awaiting orders.

"Sir, we expect the mist to stay over the ocean near El Catraz island. The sentries report no activity for the past few hours. It is possible we will not see an attack today." Nelson's mechanical arm whirred and klunked as he moved it over the papers on the table in front of him.

"I have very good reason to believe the attack will come today. I expect the Indians will attack from all sides, perhaps simultaneously, so expect to see many Indians on horseback riding up the shore from the West, where that Shell eater tribe is located. Are the civilians staying inside, as they were instructed?", Nelson asked.

"Yes, sir. They have enough provisions to last them at least 3 days. After that, we will have to open the gates to do a supply run."

"That will be unnecessary. I will end this incursion the moment it begins and prove to the President that I am not insane. I will prove that I was right all along about these heathen redskins and their crazy-as-hell leader! What of Stephens and his lot, any word?", he grimaced.

"No sir. We were expecting him to invade days ago, but nothing has happened."

"No doubt Black and his Shadowmen found him and killed him. So much the better, he is the last one that knows about my Court Martial." Nelson glared around the group, looking for any sign of reluctance or apprehension, but found only looks of fear.

"Go to your posts and stay alert with your men. When the call to defend is given, you will show no quarter. All, listen men, *ALL* Indians are to be killed on sight, do you understand?"

"General, the sound of trees falling in the forest was heard by one of our patrols near the Southern wall!" With a crisp salute, the officers departed the table, one of them pausing briefly to ask, "What of the Japanese girl, sir?"

"As far as I am concerned, she is allied with Stephens and his scurvy lot. If you see any of them, shoot them on sight. We shall outlast this day, gentlemen. I swear it!", Nelson cried out. Dismissed, the officers went to their posts to await the inevitable.

The sentries posted on the eastern wall ran into position, seeing movement in the forest below. Their guns were trained below the tree line, waiting for the slightest hint of a glint from the barrel of a gun or one of the feathers from a horse, but these were Shadowmen, their movements had such stealth that it was almost as if they were shadows themselves. The eerie silence was suddenly broken by a shrill whistle and an arrow going straight through Private Matthias' gun sight and into his right eye, killing him instantly. As his body fell, his fellow soldiers began shooting in the direction the arrow came from. They only had a moment of wild shots, though, because their enemies soon made themselves known. All one thousand of them.

General Nelson relayed orders between posts at different positions across the base, his voice just barely being heard over the recurring gun fire and arrows flying overhead. One even landed within feet of his command table. For good measure, he lifted his mechanical arm and loaded a short-range type missile-type bullet into a chamber in his lower arm. Before he could launch it, it jammed. On cue, a short wiry-haired, bespectacled man emerged from the command tent, adjusting his foggy glasses and twitching his bushy white moustache in curiosity.

"General", he hemmed, a thick German accent punctuating each word, "You think perhaps it is not yet ready for that feature, yes?"

"Puckey, Professor. I want to send our 'friends' over the wall a little gift. Use that brain of yours and fix this monstrosity you so keenly installed on me.", Nelson said, looking his mechanical arm over.

The Professor was always happy to tinker and tinker he did, adjusting gears here, tightening wires and hoses there. In just a few minutes, the General lifted his bulky arm, clicked the firing primer and with a loud bang, the bullet flew through the air and landed three feet in front of him, taking a nice chunk of ground along with it and making General Nelson and The Professor scrambling for cover.

"Perhaps it isn't ready yet, Professor."

"A few more adjustments may be necessary?", the Professor asked, scratching his head.

"Do what you must when you can, I have a war to win." The Professor gleefully ran inside the command tent to retrieve more tools and supplies while the General looked up. One of his seconds stood at attention, a look of confused fear painted on his as he looked at the small crater mere feet in front of the General.

The ships on the harbor were just as busy as the soldiers inside The Presidio. The attack was planned perfectly, with many canoes filled with Shadowmen firing their glowing energy arrows onto the decks of awaiting US Coast Guard vessels turning their guns onto them. For every canoe they blew out of the water, another five would replace them.

Across the water on El Catraz island, Raven Black watched with anticipation as he sent wave after wave of canoe boats towards the fortress. His orders were to destroy or debilitate the ships on the docks. Under no circumstances were the Shadowmen to permit the ships to make it past the wake line around the harbor. Aboard the Coast Guard Cutter Washington, seamen rushed back and forth between cannons, providing ammunition to the loaders and clearing away any duds, shrapnel or dead bodies that littered the decks. Captain Albrecht flinched as an arrow flew past him and embedded itself in the ship's bow behind him.

Disgruntled, he shifted his uniform and shouted, "Keep those bastards busy, boys! Cannon squad, make sure you keep those guns full, don't underestimate these red bastards!" "Sir, we think they're more purple now than red." A gunner corrected.

Albrecht spit in protest, "Just as bad." as another arrow spit past him and into the floor below. It hit with a thud and Albrecht's eyes opened in horror as the arrow pulsed. Before he could give the order to abandon ship, an explosion ripped through the ship's bow, sending Albrecht and the gun crew on deck sprawling through the air.

Just across the harbor, another Captain on a small tugboat winced as he saw bodies and debris flying through the air and into the ocean.

"That was a bad one, that was. We'd best get ourselves to the harbor, boys. Our friends need our help!"

A greenhorn looked at the Captain with fear, dropping the rope he had just looped over his shoulder.

"Captain Harrington, sir, you don't mean we're going to fight, do you? We have no weapons and we're just a small tugboat! What can we possibly do against that kind of firepower?"

"Get that rope up from the deck, Greenhorn! And don't you worry about what we'll do. You just follow your Captain's orders, I'll take care of the rest! I've got a friend to help!"

The deck of the small ship came alive with activity as Harrington's crew cleared the deck and prepared themselves for whatever the Captain had up his meaty, hairy sleeve.

Back on El Catraz island, Raven Black listened as one of his war chiefs updated him on the attack on the fortress.

"We managed to take out more than half of the sharpshooters on the Eastern Wall, Lord Black. It will be a matter of moments before we can shoot out the ladders."

Black's face, now more a leathery, blackened mask, a combination of a raven and man than human. His lips, a dark orange, were the only part that still resonated some humanity, spread with a sickening smile. "Do not shoot our ladders over the wall until our flight unit gives the go ahead. We are still awaiting word from the victory ship that I sent to Ongtupqa. Are our 'guests' comfortable?" Black asked, looking back to one of the tents behind him. Five strong guards surrounded the tent like statues.

"Yes, sire.", the war chief answered, sending and receiving a nod from one of the guards.

"Does the enemy know we have them? It could play to our advantage.", the guard asked.

Black shook his head and pointed to the sky. "The advantage, my brother, will come from the skies. Those are merely my feast after our great victory. Surely this country's President Grant will not want his beloved Captain Lance Stephens and the brave group from New Liberty to perish. He will give me the territories I demand or I will kill all of them and claim more white eye camps for our cause. How many white eye have come to the way of Shadow?"

The chief responded in negative, showing Black one of the magic stones that he himself gave them to convert Nelson's soldiers with. "The stones will not work on the white eye soldiers, Master. We do not understand, but they will not turn completely. Even when we do get them to turn, the conversion will not hold."

"That cannot be possible. Did you do exactly as I instructed?", Black seethed, grabbing his chief by the scruff of his jacket.

The chief blabbered, "Yes, sire! I swear I did everything you asked! They will not turn!"

Black released his hold and sent the chief back into the fray. He could not understand why the stones were not working on the Americans. He knew they had worked before during the battle of Fort Francisco. The only explanation had to be that Nelson figured a way around it. Or perhaps the problem was Nelson himself. Smiling again, he called over to a group of Shadowmen kneeling in a circle in front of a glowing, purple flame. Each of the men had unique war paint on their faces: Their skin was just as purple and black as their brethren, however, the paint that could be seen on their faces was maroon, outlined with an almost orange-like border. The pattern followed their cheek lines and eyes. Each of them seemed to glide over to their leader and stood at attention as he laid out his orders.

"I have a special assignment for you, my warriors of the Raven. Your time has come. You are to infiltrate the compound of The Presidio and bring to me the metal man. He is to live, do you understand? Bring him to me alive."

No response was given other than their mysterious disappearance into the misty air.

"My lord Raven, all is happening as you have foretold. The champion of the light is dead and we are within the reach of victory. Finally, my people will have a future free of the white eye, brought forth by the wings of the Raven!" Almost as if by his words, several large shadows moved across the island below, cast by six massive behemoths of war flying high above. The Raven's Flight had arrived.

Squads of soldiers emptied their bullets into the seemingly endless swathes of Shadowmen pouring into the walls of the Presidio's walls on all sides. The Eastern wall was the hardest hit, having taken too many direct strikes by the magical arrows. It would only be too soon before a few more minor explosions by those horrifyingly powerful weapons made an opening for Black's forces below.

The Northern Harbor was equally pressed, taking losses dearly, each ship the Coast Guard had sent towards the war canoes had been shockingly laid to waste. Captain Alex Diaz watched, stunned that another Cutter sustained a direct hit to its lower water line, exploding metal and wood, leaving the ship to sink slowly, along with its men, to a watery grave. He had no time to mourn the loss of his sister vessels, though, for he saw a terrible sight bearing down upon him from across the bay: A ship that was easily twice the size of the Guard's biggest Cutter to date.

"A dreadnaught!", he cried out. It looked to be made of some kind of hardened metal, shaped like a wide canoe, but not as narrow along the bow and stern. He did not see a mast, however he could see rows of oars on either side, indicating a crew of oarsmen below decks. Along the hull of the ship, he saw rivets bulleted in shape and pattern, crisscrossing across all sides, holding it together, he assumed. On her deck, Diaz could make out several turrets arranged throughout, but instead of being loaded with cannons, they were loaded with huge arrows! It was like nothing he had ever seen. Normally, he would laugh at such a sight, but after seeing the damage the smaller versions of those same arrows could do, he feared for what carnage came from these monsters.

"Aim for those turrets, we cannot allow those damn things to be fired towards any of our ships! We need to turn the damn tide, hell if I'm gonna lose to some damned reddies!" The men loaded the howitzers on deck and aimed towards the monster ship, however, being unaccustomed to being moved to different targets, it made the aim difficult, compounded with the grim fact that they were on the water. Run that engine and make us cross that wake line! I want to get to El Catraz and end this! Don't wait for my order, you fire at will!"

The gunners cranked the lever on the howitzer and the massive cannon roared as it blasted at the oncoming ship. The cannonball flew through the air and towards the ship, landing squarely on the quarterdeck. The Captain and men on the Cutter yelled out in victory but they quickly saw the terrible truth. The cannonball did indeed hit the ship, but it merely made a dent in the hull, not enough to poke a hole.

"What the hell is that ship made of?!", Diaz spat.

In response to their attack, the Shadowmen's ship aimed their huge arrow gun to the American ship and fired their payload, a group of arrows the length of a horse and almost half as wide as a cannon itself. The arrows split in midair and flew like missiles towards the ship. Amazingly, the metallic shaft of the arrows did not weigh them down, instead almost seeming to cause them to go faster. The Captain bellowed for his men to dive to the deck as the arrows, one by one, landed on different areas of the ship, one below the water line, another near the mast.

"Too damned close", Diaz blew through his mustache in anger. "Where's our damn brig?!", he called out to one of his midshipmen. The boy looked about the ocean and called out in victorious relief as an explosive force tore through several of the smaller Shadow canoeships. The Navy had finally come, led by the most unusually small tugboat Stein had ever seen. The Captain looked through his scope at the Signaling Officer on the Brig across the bay. Through Morse Code, the Acting Signal Officer on the Brig instructed Diaz they would lead the fleet towards the island where the enemy ships were originating from.

"That's our opening! Lay the course and follow that Brig! We're hammering the bastards through!"

Back at El Catraz, a small black raven landed atop a large perch in front of Black's command tent. A guard looked on in fear and awe as it transformed itself into Raven Black.

"The Navy has brought its monster out just in time to match with our monster. What is the word on our warriors along the walls?", Black asked.

"Sire, we have breached the Eastern Wall and the ladders have been fired over the gap."

"Excellent. The ravens should be arriving at the fortress just about now."

The guard was about to leave when the large shadow of one of Black's dirigibles appeared on the ground near him.

"Perfect, our unit arrived from the Canyon! As soon as the Captain of that vessel lands, relay orders to send it over the waters to attack any ships approaching our island."

Black's smug expression changed suddenly when the anchor line from the dirigible landed squarely on his guard, killing and impaling him instantly. Before he could yell in protest, an arrow shot at him and would have struck him had he not used his supernatural agility to dodge.

"What is the meaning of this treachery?", he demanded.

In response, Sen-hi Sakeda and Shaman Spirit Bear repelled and landed on the ground in front of him. "You have a great deal to answer for, son of darkness!" Sen-hi said, looking at Raven Black through eyes of pure rage. Black could not believe what he was seeing.

"I sent two groups of well-trained Shadow Warriors, powerful and indestructible! How did you survive?" The Shaman responded, "My old friend, you should know there is no weapon that darkness can use that the light cannot break."

"Traitor, that is all you are to me!", Black accused.

Sen-hi quickly positioned herself between the two men but the Shaman butted his medicine staff in front of her, causing Black to step back in surprise.

"No, young one. Your job is to free the prisoners from that tent. I will take care of my friend here."

"How do you plan on doing that?", she asked.

"With skill and luck, child. But mostly with this.", the Shaman pointed at his head, eliciting a nod from his companion, who ran straight for the prisoner tent behind Black's own tent. The two old friends circled each other, unsure of what the other would do.

"So, 'friend', how will you hurt me? Will you stab me in the back, like you did when you ran off? All those times I could have used your advice. Will you pierce me right in this powerful magic heart, a holy gift from the Raven himself?"

"That 'gift', is your slave collar, my brother.", Spirit Bear said simply.

"Do not call me brother!", Raven Black screamed, loosing his saber from his belt notch.

With unchecked anger, he brought it down upon Shaman Spirit Bear, who brought up his staff to block. The two weapons clanged in protest of each other. Black reeled slightly from the sound, knowing that the sword should have cut the Shaman's staff into a hundred splintered pieces.

"There are more holy things on this island than you know of, Raven Black." The two continued their struggle while Sen-hi approached the tent, sword drawn.

The five guards were already in formation, ready to strike given the opportunity. Sen-hi knew immediately how to dispatch them. Large groups were, after all, her specialty.

In one single stroke, she sheathed her sword, kneeled and uttered, "Sakeda Ryu, Mantu Ryu Sen!" Sen-hi uses her back and hips to spring up into the air, unsheathing her sword and, with godlike accuracy and speed, cuts across the air and through the guards with one solid stroke. She then lands right in front of the tent's entrance, sword sheathed and standing, her back turned, knowing the sound that would come next. Five thuds in solid succession followed, all of the guards landed on the floor dead instantly. Inside the tent, Sen-hi saw nothing but masks on the wall and a fire pit and some blankets on the floor, similar to how Bright Dusk would arrange the main hub of New Liberty and his living hut. She wondered where the prisoners were but also why he would post five guards outside an empty tent.

Her answer came at the end of a fast, foreboding sound. That of a low hissing noise that was coming from somewhere near the back of the tent. "A trap!" she cried out, scrambling to escape, but before she could get out, the tent exploded with a tremendous force, sending her flying past two tents and into a larger tent across the way.

Back inside the walls of The Presidio, it was all the soldiers could do to quell the oncoming hordes spilling into the large cavity that now existed on the upper level of the wall. Shadowmen piled into the wall's second level, dodging hails of bullets, while a secondary group on a platform attached to some of the ladders shot volleys of energy-tipped arrows into the fray above. The soldiers were forced to fight hand-to-hand, using their bayonets, knives or even sabers, if they had them. But they were little to no match for the seasoned, experienced and bloodthirsty Shadow Tribe. These warriors were ravenous, chaotic in their attack postures and tactics, employing brute force and gouge-level theatrics whenever possible. The American infantry were accustomed to fighting Indians, but not like these fought. These were not the typical scalping, hooting groups of brightly-colored warriors they used to fight. These men wielded swords made of the sharpest, most vicious metal, that could slash through skin like paper, their barbaric movements, techniques and methods stunned the soldiers who are so used to fighting in a uniform manner. "Don't let the bastards intimidate you! Form your lines and don't forget your training! We won't let them have this base! Not the Presidio!"

A soldier mustered up his courage upon hearing an officer yell out the motivational message behind him, pushing further and further against the hordes of warriors gaining onto their lines. But they were stopping them somehow. Some spilled onto the ledge, some even jumped down into the lower level, but they would be stopped...at great cost, but they were stopped. The Presidio was holding the Shadow Tribe back dearly, but it was holding them back.

The darkness cleared and gave way to the sight of the same island Sen-hi landed on with her companion, Shaman Spirit Bear. Slowly, she rose from the rubble that she landed in and checked herself for any injuries. She was not disappointed. Her hakama had been torn and bloodied from the explosion, bits of shrapnel were hanging off her skin like small tags. Slowly she inspected her sword, which normally would have been unusable, but because of its special qualities, was un-damaged. The sheath's normally dark red color was blackened with ash. Her eye patch was no longer on her right eye and she could feel a deep scar running down the very same eye she had been injured on before. The wound, apparently, had re-opened. She felt some blood on her face, but not enough to be life-threatening, she was surprised to discover. Looking around her, she saw the reason. Just as the bomb went off and she dove for cover, a funny thing happened. Her foot caught the lip of one of the Shadowmen's shields that was leaning against the wall of the tent and it fell right in front of her body and in the path of the explosion. Enough to propel her away and still cause some damage, but not enough to kill, the shield saved her life.

Sen-hi laughed to herself, not sure whether to thank the gods or sheer luck that she survived so violent an explosion. In the distance, she saw the Shaman and his old friend fight and her bushido told her not to interfere. Not yet. She suddenly heard some cries high above and followed the sounds to a dirigible floating slowly away from the island overhead. Using a passing bird as a tool, Sen-hi reached and saw that inside the floating ship, a small group of people were fighting for their lives against an overwhelming force of Shadow Warriors. Among the group was Captain Stephens, Bright Dusk, Chen Xien, Lieutenant Steele and some other members of New Liberty. Behind the warriors that were fighting her friends were two figures: Raven Black's son, Right Hand, and the devilish Macarthur, the man that she first met when she had arrived in San Francisco. She needed no further motivation and ran with all her might, tying her sheathed sword to what was left of her belt and grabbing the Adistan.

She raised it to the sky and reached with her mind, willing it to become what she needed it to be, just like Sasquatch told her. When she opened her eyes, she was gleefully amazed that it had become a huge Kyudo bow, with a grappling arrow as ammunition. A nearby horse would serve as her transport as she rode with haste closer to the balloon ship. Sen-hi thanked the spirit of her Father for teaching her the ways of The Samurai and Kyudo as she tied on a rope to the grapple and leveled the bow and arrow towards the keel of the ship high above her at a gut-wrenching 500 feet.

Even for a master Fletcher, the distance between her and the ship would be impossible to meet, but she had the way of Sakeda on her side.

She adjusted for height, wind speed and velocity and let loose, yelling "Sakeda Kyudo Ryu, Yatto No Yajirushi!"

The arrow and rope soared through the sky with amazing speed, impossibly towards the flying ship and landed exactly on point. Sen-hi instinctively grabbed hold of the end of the rope, tied hard to the Kyudo bow and hung on for her life as she also flew through the air and towards the fight of her life.

The monstrous Shadow Tribe's dreadnaught, as Captain Diaz called it, coasted across the bay towards The Presidio, making any American vessel near it look like toy boats, both in size and strength. It wasn't until The Brig arrived, it more than matched its enemy's prowess. Armed with eighteen cannonades and two long guns, the square-rigged, two-masted warship turned its starboard battery side to the dreadnaught, firing squad primed on the target. "Starboard battery, aim for the mizzenmast! Fire!" The cannons fired each in succession, an ear-splitting concussive repetition of force loosing a barrage of damaging cargo towards the other ship. The captain of the dreadnaught, Two Moons, yelled for his men to jump to the deck as the ship's plating and mast were reduced to holey debris. The Brig's crew cried in victory, but Captain Diaz quieted them down.

"Reload and prepare to fire again. They aren't beaten yet, not a ship that size."

Diaz gave the order to come to port, giving the enemy time to recover until the next attack. Two Moons had little experience leading a ship's crew. It took him several weeks before he could stop losing his stomach whilst on deck. If it weren't for the traitor white eye, Macarthur, who had some knowledge of sailing, he would never have known how to steer, let alone lead a crew.

"They are turning, brothers. Aim our remaining cannons at their broadside as they turn. Fire!", Macarthur commanded. More loud booms filled the smoky air, followed by a volley of cannonballs flying at the Brig, some landing in the water near her side, a few skipping across the top of the ship's borderline. Diaz's ship had already turned to port by the time the dreadnaught finished firing and they let go another barrage from their port side, some of the payload hit below the mast but not enough to make it give. The rest struck ahead of the water line.

"She's giving dearly, gents. Keep on it and don't give 'em an inch of breathing room! Come to starboard! Starboard battery, you'd best have those cannons ready when we come to target range!"

The Gunnery Officers relayed his commands as expected, the stray shots of riflemen from the crow's nests of the dreadnaught peppering the Brig's deck as it came about starboard.

Silent Eagle knew how this would end and decided it was the best opportunity to use the weapon his master gave him in case he was in this predicament. Running across the deck, he came to the main mast and cranked a wooden lever that was attached to it.

As the Brig turned for another attack, Silent Eagle smiled, blood trailing from his lips as he said, "This will decide things."

Just across the water, Diaz's men were primed and ready to lay hooks for board and capture of the enemy vessel when a loud noise shook the waters around them. Both ships shivered under the intensity of the object that was emerging from the hold of the Shadow Tribe's dreadnaught.

"What is that thing, Captain?"

"I don't know, but whatever it is, we have to destroy it at any cost." Diaz responded as he surveyed the object and couldn't understand what he was looking at.

It had the shape of a cannon, but where the actual muzzle of the barrel's hole should be, an odd shaped device could be seen covering it. It looked like a circle with a strange pattern weaved, actually weaved, around the different sections of the outer circle with metal. This made the circular cap or whatever it was look like it was giving the cannon's barrels a web for a cover or shield of some sort. Diaz came to the conclusion that it did not matter what it was to be used for and gave the order to board an capture the vessel.

Immediately, the hooks flew over and latched on to the Shadow Tribe's ship. In a flurry of gun fire and arrows flying overhead, the men of both ships fought with abandon, the clanging of saber and bayonet, rifle fire from overhead and arrows whistling across the sky was deafening.

Just as Diaz dispatched another man, he turned and there in front of him was the Captain, Two Moons. "Surrender, we have you out manned and out gunned!"

"Do you? My tribe-brother was one of the men your men killed in that cave you white eye army men investigated. I promised to avenge him and so I shall!" With a motion of his hands, Silent Eagle gave the order and before Diaz could do anything, a loud hum vibrated through the ship. The shaking was so intense, it brought Diaz and most of everyone onboard to their knees or on their rears.

"What the devil? What is this evil?", Diaz recoiled.

"Your race's end, white eye.", Silent Eagle said flatly.

From the tugboat's cabin, Captain Harrington's attention was diverted to the battle on the dreadnaught by one of his men. He looked through his scope and froze in terror at what he saw. The strange weapon onboard the Indian's ships was glowing with a powerfully intense purple light and was shaking like some monster about to roar...and roar it did.

In a sound akin to a raven's cry, the weapon unleashed a blast of dark light that enveloped the Indian's ship and the Brig aside it. The water that the ships were on crashed upwards in massive waves so big that anyone watching from a distance would have sworn a freak tidal wave was coming their way. Harrington turned his little ship to port instinctively and even though he was a safe distance away from the explosion, could still feel the shockwave from the blast, whatever it was.

"Captain, what the hell was that? Is the Brig still afloat, sir?"

"Doubtful anything could have survived that blast, greenhorn. How many canoe ships are left between us and El Catraz?", Harrington asked, looking through the chaos.

"None, sir. When they saw the Brig enter the harbor, they focused their attention on that ship and were all last seen near...that blast."

Harrington looked ahead and saw that the island was within reach. He smiled but only slightly, his smile turning to a solemn frown, thinking how Diaz and his crew died valiantly as a distraction so that he and the rest of the cutters could make it to the island and stop the attack at the Presidio.

As he was giving the orders to lay anchor and disembark on the island, he noticed two large airships flying towards the fortress across the bay.

One of his men aimed a rifle at one of the ships, calling out, "Sir, I see someone hanging from a rope attached to one of the ships. Shall I fire?"

Harrington took a closer look through his scope and laughed, "Put your weapon down, swab. That crazy gal hanging from that ship up there be our only hope to end this war!"

Aboard one of the airships flying towards the Presidio, Captain Stephens, Bright Dusk and Lieutenant Chris Steele were being held at bay by a large group of armed Shadow Tribesmen. The purple-colored warriors were inching closer to the New Liberty group, spears getting dangerously close, while at the same time Stephens and his friends could see themselves getting closer to the edge of the airship.

"I thought you were this master sword fighter, Stephens.", Steele quipped, attempting to bat away one of the spears, just out of arms reach.

"You see any swords around, let me know."

"Always with excuses but never a real solution, Captain.", a voice said.

The group turned in surprise as a figure leapt, amazingly, from underneath the airship and right in front of the Shadowmen. Bright Dusk's eyes smiled in relief when he realized who it was.

"Sen-hi! We thought you and brother Spirit Bear dead!"

"That old fool is as wily as a tanuki!", she smiled.

The Shadowmen looked at each other in confusion, not sure what to make of this new intruder. Sen-hi quickly put her hand to her sword and was about to attack when she noticed it did not come out. "You'll be stubborn now, will you?", she said out loud, thinking the sword was telling her this particular situation did not merit its use.

"Looks like you are having trouble with your weapon, foreigner!", Loud Wolf laughed, urging his men onward. They quickly charged towards her, spears extended and ready to impale their enemy. Sen-hi, however, was not that easy to kill. In a flash, she took out another weapon, a sword in fact, cut all of their spears in half.

"I do not have to use Sakeda Ryu to defeat you lot.", she revealed, tossing the sword to Captain Stephens as she took a kenpo stance.

"What the hell is that, some kind of weird dance? We are warriors of shadow! We will destroy you and your dancing!"

The 10 Shadowmen rushed Sen-hi as she weaved in and out of their attacks, one at a time. Her movements were so fluid, so perfect, it was almost as if she could see where their fists and legs would end up before they got there. Throughout their efforts, she managed to land several successive blows to their abdomens, knee caps, ribs and throats, causing half of them to go down almost immediately upon rushing her. The other half of the group that rushed her picked up their broken spears and thrust at her with the cracked part of their weapons.

She was ready for this and used her lower arms and elbows to deflect any oncoming stabs and thrusts. She even used judo techniques to unbalance her attackers and send many of them over the edge. Now it was just her and Loud Wolf, who was standing in front of her trembling in fear, a fresh stream of urine trickling down his pants.

"You can either stand there in a puddle of your own fear or surrender to my friends, the choice is yours."

Loud Wolf looked around and then smiled as he looked across them. "I think I'll take the other exit, my dear."

Sen-hi followed his eyes to the other airship that was already above the Presidio, its huge guns trained on key buildings and the hordes of people below in the civilian section. Sen-hi wasted no time and ran with all her might used her sword, which now decided to answer her, to cut one of the ropes attached to the dirigible's airbag.

She grabbed the rope tightly and yelled, "Stephens, throw me the sword I gave you!" The Captain looked confused but complied. As she caught it, it turned back into the grappling hook and Kyudo bow she had earlier.

A moment later, her rope could be seen travelling through the sky and landing squarely on the other airship's outer hull. Sen-hi ran the rest of the way and jumped off the airship. On the deck of the other airship, the Captain noticed a slight weight on the ship.

Just as he was about to give the order, one of his men called out, "Sir, there's a...girl! A woman, that sword woman is hanging off our ship!"

Right Hand could not believe it and had to see it for himself. There indeed was Sen-hi, hanging off a rope that had somehow been affixed to his airship!

"She won't be there for long, I think.", he said, taking out his dagger and cutting at the rope. Below, Sen-hi saw him and un-sheathed her sword.

"Sakeda Ryu, Taifuu no Ken!" In a mighty gust of air from her swing, she was lifted, actually lifted, the full length of her rope onto the deck of Right Hand's airship. Landing on her feet, her and Right Hand's eyes met, an air of synergistic energy flowed between them.

"How's the eye, foreigner?", Right Hand chuckled, tapping at his own eye.

"Do not fret, I shall repay you for that 'gift'."

Right Hand dismissed his men to their stations, ordering them to begin loading the guns and aiming them below.

"I implore you to see reason and surrender to me now, Right Hand, son of Proud Eagle, now Raven Black. You are outmatched in my presence."

Right Hand laughed maniacally, taking out his saber and striking what looked like a very stalwart defensive stance.

"I shall show you how 'outmatched' I am in comparison to you, my beauty."

The two rushed at each other, Sen-hi deciding to go for an all-out fencing battle rather than rely on power-based techniques. Their swords hit more metal than skin, the force of their charges causing each of them to push back and hit opposing sides of the airship's prow. Right Hand swiped away some cold sweat from his brow and pursued at Sen-hi with a flurry of strikes. Sen-hi brought up her hilt to counter, but could only defend against a few of them. Right Hand's face contorted in gleeful victory as he saw the stream of blood that was now flowing from the wound he caused across her arm. Sen-hi jumped back and grabbed at her wounded arm, pressing down hard to constrict the blood flow.

"I won't give you a chance to recover!", he cried out, lunging at her with all his force. Sen-hi quickly dodged his lunge and went to counter strike, but hit the back of his armor, doing little damage to the leather encasing her opponent. A loud clanking sound signaled that the cannons were ready to fire upon the buildings below. Sen-hi knew she had precious little time before the unsuspecting innocents below would be killed.

"You leave me no choice."

"What nonsense are you prattling on about now, woman?"

"Your Shaman asked me not to take your life or that of your Father's, but I see no other alternative to stopping those cannons. I only hope he forgives me for what I am about to do." Neglecting her bleeding arm, she positioned herself for another strike and Right Hand cried out in glee, drunk with battle fever. He rushed at her, saber rattling and eyes wide with madness.

Sen-hi closed her eyes as he ran towards her, breathing slowly and then, just before exhaling, "Sakeda Ryu, Ken No Tabi."

In one movement, she sheathed and then...nothing. Her sword would not come back out of the sheath! The son of Raven Black took this opportunity and rammed his saber at her vulnerable body but hit metal instead. Just as he was about to speak, he could feel a chilling sensation come over him. In an instant, his body knew real pain and he saw the color of his new skin bleed out along with the blood that was now being drained from his body from a wound made by a sword. A sword that was held by Captain Lance Stephens.

Unceremoniously, the Captain removed his sword from Right

Hand's chest and turned towards Sen-hi as the once proud Mapiyan warrior fell to the floor, dying in a pool of his own blood. Sen-hi was still trembling, still in the stance of Ken No Tabi, as Captain Stephens slowly stood her up.

"My sword...it would not answer me. It would not answer me when I needed it most. This has never happened, not this many times. Lance...this has never..."

Stephens threw down his sword and brought her to him, kissing her deeply. Sen-hi could feel his arms around her, his eyes boring into hers with passion and, love, it was there, too. All this time these two warriors were bitter rivals and even enemies at one point but after all the plotting, strategizing and exchanging looks of contempt, she realized that there was real love behind it all, even though it was almost impossible for he to see.

They parted and looked at each other as if for the first time.

"I thought you might need help. Even a master of Sakeda Ryu needs help once in a while.", he said.

Sen-hi's face was flush with tears; whether they were tears of defeat from her sword's uncooperative behavior or his words, she was not sure.

"I am done.", she finally uttered, her body becoming limp in his arms. Determinedly, he hoisted her onto a crate on deck.

"Right now, Raven Black is down there, having taken our friend, the Shaman, hostage. He means to take over this base from Nelson and use it as a tool against the United States. Sen-hi, there aren't enough men to stop him, let alone get to him, but I can lower you right in his path. You can stop him before he opens the gate and allows his men waiting on the Southern section inside."

"Lance, you saw what happened. My sword will not answer me. It will not see Raven Black's death as a means for justice to be done. I cannot stop him."

"Sen-hi, you do not have to kill someone in order to stop them. I wonder if your sword would answer you if your mind was open to other choices. Perhaps the problem is not bringing justice to Raven Black, but rather, bringing justice to the world he represents.", he surmised.

Sen-hi's face looked more sure now, but he could see some confusion still painted on her eyes.

"If his men could see their glorious leader defeated by a, forgive me, 'mere woman', they would definitely lose faith in him and break ranks. That would give some time for a counter offensive from within.", he said.

"From within? What do you mean?", she asked.

"Let me worry about that part." Tying a rope to her and giving her the Adistan, he pointed downward to a large mass of Shadow Men converging on the civilian section from a massive breach along the Eastern Wall. At the front was Raven Black and another man, tied up and being pushed along at spear point: Spirit Bear. "Send me to him!", Sen-hi roared, the fire of will again alive in her eyes. As she braced for the all-too-familiar sensation of flying through the air by way of the grappling hook and bow, she could almost faintly hear a voice in her head. A voice of acceptance.

Raven Black marched to victory with his army of strong Shadow Men behind him. He had been victorious in his assault on the Presidio, capturing General Nelson, laying waste to more than half of his men in the process, disabling the American fleet and along with it any hope of rescue for them and now, he was about to unleash the final blow. In the rows of buildings in front of him hid scores of scared white eyes; Mothers, Brothers, Sisters, Grandmothers and Grandfathers. All manner of people that, for some reason, could not fight and were sent here for safety. But in the world of the Shadow, safety was for the weak. Anyone not fighting alongside their brothers were as good as the dust they trampled upon for fear of their lives. A groan coming from his one-time friend, now traitor about to die, Spirit Bear, made him scoff in amusement.

"You are about to witness the end of this base's usefulness, my 'friend'. The white eye thought to use this as a headquarters and main attack point against us but look, I have usurped them and will turn this once proud fortress into rubble!"

As if on cue, several siege tanks were driven into range from behind Black and his honor guard. It was terribly ironic, Black thought, that the very tanks used to protect the people now inside the buildings would be used to exact his revenge on them for their masters' sins. Black lifted his arm to give the order to fire and was stopped mid-sentence by a loud explosion behind him. He turned and saw, impossibly, Sen-hi Sakeda standing atop what used to be a siege tank, now just a crumbling smoking pile of metal.

"If you want something to aim your machines of vengeance at, Raven Black, here I am." He could not believe it but there she was.

"I had sent my best men against you and this traitor and you survived. You were blown to bits by my trap at the island, and you survived. You flew like a damned thunderbird at my son's airship and no doubt fought him. You fought my son and his men, and survived!", he gritted his teeth.

"Your son died of his own foolish actions, driven by madness and run through by the sword of a man better than I."

Her words did not reach him. Fueled by anger and hatred, driven by the lust for power, Raven Black ordered his men to stand down and took out his saber, leveling it at Sen-hi.

"Your old friend Macarthur told me a great deal about you Samurai before I killed him."

Sen-hi's heart skipped a beat, angered for wanting to kill the man who imprisoned her herself.

"I know all about your method of fighting, girl. I know how that blade works and I tell you this now, you will never kill me. Even if you want to, that wonderful weapon will not allow it.", Black smiled victoriously.

"Then I will kill the idea of you." Sen-hi answered, sheathing her sword and positioning herself in a stance. "I don't know any special attacks or spells to use, but I do know this.", Raven Black said, taking his saber. He then began to prance in a circle in front of her, making whooping sounds and cries of an indecipherable nature.

As he stomped around, Sen-hi could detect an aura of darkness emanating from his heart, the stone the Shaman told her about, and enveloping his body. The moment he was covered, he lunged at her, saber raised, and crashed down upon her. It was all she could do to dodge as Black's attack crashed down on the ground she had just stood on, making a small crater.

"You see, girl? You see the power of the Raven? The power of the Shadow?"

Sen-hi positioned herself again and looked at the ground, then his heart stone, "All I see is a hole that needs to be fixed. Sakeda Ryu, Kaze No Hitofuki!" With a side swipe of the flat of her blade, she created a powerful gust of wind that sent debris and some of the tank's shrapnel flying towards Black, who tried dodging some of the larger pieces, which landed around and behind him.

He rushed towards her, his saber connecting with her sword, sending sparks flying around the battlefield. The Shaman gasped in awe and was then distracted by a large commotion behind him. Several groups of Shadow Men were suddenly engaged in close combat with a huge number of infantry. One of them approached the Shaman and released him. He was relieved when he noticed the soldier was, in fact, Bright Dusk in military uniform. The two men embraced in relief of seeing each other alive and turned their attention to the struggle in front of them. "Our reinforcements finally arrived via a brand new steam-powered locomotive transport President Grant sent our way." He motioned to the soldiers now engaged in combat with Black's remaining warriors and honor guards." Bright Dusk turned and saw his New Liberty companion fighting her own battle.

"Sen-hi seems to have the upper hand in the fight, Brother Spirit Bear."

"It is an even fight, brother. For even if Raven Black knows no Samurai fighting tactics, he still knows how to fight as a tribal warrior and that should be enough to make him a credible threat against her."

Another powerful strike from Black's obsidian blade sent Sen-hi reeling backwards, hitting one of the now unoccupied tanks. She did not have time to react to the sting of the hard metal on her back for Black was again on the offensive, waving his saber above his head so as to confuse her to his method of attack. She tried positioning herself for the ultimate attack of Sakeda Ryu, the Ken No Tabi, but the supersonic strikes, lunges and dodges that Black was implementing made it impossible for her to make any headway. To make matters worse, the wound on her arm had re-opened and gave her a slight disadvantage in the draw of her sword.

"Shadow Tribe special attack, Raven's Claw!" Black cackled, mocking Sen-hi's own battle cries as he rushed upon her with impossible speed. The range of this attack was too close for dodging, so she took up her sheath to block and missed. Black speared her thigh, causing a huge gash to appear. Sen-hi cried out in ear-splitting pain, dropping to one knee in a puddle of her own blood.

Bright Dusk immediately rushed to her aide, but she raised a hand in protest. "No! I do this myself!"

The Shaman was about to protest himself but their attention was brought to two honor guards who broke from the fray to deal with them personally. Bright Dusk reluctantly turned from his badly-wounded companion's side and jumped into battle alongside Spirit Bear.

Raven Black paced in front of his damaged opponent. He could not think of a better position for her to be in.

"The Champion of Light." He scoffed, "More like the defeated weakling of Light. Do you not see it is folly to continue, Sen-hi?"

Enraged and moving by sheer willpower, she jumped at him, sword slashing wildly but cutting nothing but air or meeting his blade as he easily parried her now extremely weakened strikes.

"Come now, I am not an unfeeling animal. I will grant you mercy and end your life painlessly. Think of it as a final gift from the Raven of Shadow, the only real god of this world...Sky Woman."

"I am tired." Sen-hi breathed out, almost unable to speak from the weakness slowly setting upon her from lack of blood.

"Yes, I know. And I can end your weariness, child. Do not fret, I shall bring a new order into this world. The order that no man shall be governed but by his own choices. I think it odd that someone of your history, with all the stories of oppression, civil war and foreign involvement at your shores, should ally yourself with the murdering white eye. My alliance with the god of Shadow was a natural answer to their barbaric nature and encroaching ways. Do you honestly think the god of light would allow me to do all of this glorious carnage? No, only through the dark Raven's will can I achieve my beautiful world of chaos and disorder. Only through chaos can I achieve victory against all white men and bring about the true world of the Raven for all mankind, first here, then even your homeland and then, of course, the world itself!" Raven Black then raised his saber to deliver the final blow and stopped as he heard Sen-hi say something almost incoherently.

"Mapiya." The word was almost lost to the wind, so quietly did she utter it.

"What?", he answered, stepping closer, his sword raised again for attack.

"You never, not once mentioned your people, the Mapiya. All you spoke of was the Raven and his wishes.", she struggled to breathe.

"And what of it?", he spat.

"It speaks of your real Master, Raven Black. Your plans are not of your own making, they are a product of the dark god's sinister plot for taking over. You are merely a pawn in his nefarious plans, do you not see it? You speak of chaos but what you really mean is a world without any choice of chaos. It will not be a world ruled by men or their choices. Every man will be a puppet of the Raven, subject to his whims and desires. Even you will prove to be a useless tool and summarily disposed of when all of this is done."

Black stood before her, stammering for a response as she continued, "The governance of man is essential to his rise. Within each man is the potential for greatness, yet it be not within him to achieve that greatness whilst also supplanting another rung on the ladder of human misery. That way is folly. Your way is folly, Raven Black, and it must be stopped now at all cost. Have at thee!"

Tenderly and with great care, Sen-hi stood, positioning herself for what she knew would be her final attempt at finishing this fight. Raven Black trembled slightly at the sight of his enemy standing in front of him, knowing that it was the strength of her very spirit that caused this miracle to occur as the life blood poured out of her. Looking around him, he could see for the first time, through eyes that seemed to be coming into focus from darkness, some of his men staring at them. He shook off any doubts, knowing that he must finish this woman once and for all, for the glory of the Raven.

Raven Black let out a shrill war cry, ramming his whole body towards her, saber thrust forward and aimed straight at her heart.

All at once, with all the strength of her spirit, Sen-hi sheathed her sword and cried out, "Sakeda Ryu Ultimate Attack, Ken No Tabi!" The air between them seemed to come alive with electricity. Raven Black's sword penetrated through Sen-hi's sheath as she brought it up from the draw and just as it was about to pierce her, an amazing and impossible thing happened. The blade of Sakeda rammed itself right in the very middle of Black's saber, splitting it in two perfect halves! It did not stop there, for the rest of the attack took her blade right into the stone protecting his heart and shattered it into pieces. The force of the blow was so traumatic, that the color from Black's body was literally splattered away from him at once as he was sent flying backwards and to the ground behind him. There was a moment of stunned silence as Black's Shadow Men strained to see through the smoke and char that had surrounded Sen-hi and her opponent. The warriors dropped their weapons in shock as they saw their beloved leader lying prone on the ground in front of her.

"You did it, Sen-hi!", a familiar voice cried out, making her turn slowly. It was the man she had just fell in love with, Captain Lance Stephens.

But it was all she could do to stand and seeing him was all it took for her to finally fall, Stephens catching her gingerly in his arms as she fell unconscious. The Shaman and Bright Dusk came forward and rushed her to a makeshift infirmary that had just been raised from a downed dirigible near the center of The Presidio's courtyard.

"At least the damned things were good for something.", Harrington harrumphed, shouldering a large rifle with a massive barrel on his burly shoulder.

The sun was beginning to set as the soldiers rounded up the remaining warriors, along with Raven Black, who could be heard moaning in pain and defeat, all the way to the prison house. Upon seeing their leader dragged in defeat, the warriors quickly lost the hold of the Shadow and accepted incarceration for their crimes.

In the distance, perched atop the barrel of the tank Sen-hi destroyed earlier, a pitch black Raven surveyed its surroundings and then flapped suddenly in surprise as another Raven, one white in color, landed next to it. "You now see and understand why this was folly, brother?" The White Raven spoke, her crystalline blue eyes glistening in the setting sun's rays.

"This is only a small distraction, sister. There will be other times.", the Black Raven stated.

"Will you never tire of seeing your plans in defeat?", the White Raven asked.

"Defeat is always temporary until the next attempt, Sister. Your champion may have won here today, but I am always nearby, ready to strike at the heart of a weak spirit."

With a flap of his wings, the dark Raven god flew away into the shadows, leaving his sister behind. "That is why you will always lose, brother. For a spirit full of hope can always be a sword against any dark purpose."

With a mighty gust of wind, the White Raven flew towards the sun, giving a final ray of healing light from between its feathers onto Sen-hi, who could see it with her spirit and eyes. With both her eyes.

Holding her hand, Stephens smiled and kissed her gently.

"You have given us a great foundation on which to build our future.", he said, looking at her.

"The future we will build together.", she embraced him, holding him tight against her and knowing for the first time that this was one battle she would have to lose...and be glad to lose for the rest of her life.

EPILOGUE

The morning rays found their way inside the hastily built infirmary tent in the center of the damaged Presidio's courtyard. The wounded man awoke to a sensation of severe pain in his chest and weakness across his body. As he surveyed his body, all he could see was bandages, bruise marks and darkened patches where the stamp of ashen smoke left its mark. On the small table next to him, bottles of salves and ointments were left open and almost empty from use on him. The nurses and doctors were running back and forth through the cramped quarters of the tent, yelling for instruments he was unfamiliar with, rolls of bandages flapping in the air as the nurses with them ran towards the doctor, like some sort of victory flag. The man groaned as he stood up, then found himself having to sit back down on a chair next to his cot, subject to the searing pain he was still feeling. He had no idea how much time had passed, no knowledge of the outcome of any of the events that had transpired since Sen-hi fought with Raven Black...with him.

"I was wondering when you'd wake up.", a voice said, breaking his concentration.

Raising his head his eyes met a familiar sight, his old friend, Spirit Bear, former Man of Medicine and Shaman of their old tribe. Saying nothing, Spirit Bear's friend turned his face and raised an open palm, then pushed towards the Shaman, a sign of defeat for their people.

"That is the first time I have seen you do anything resembling a connection with our tribe and people since that fateful day in my tent. Brother Proud Spirit, are you here with me?", the Shaman asked with hope.

Tears came to his eyes as he looked at Spirit Bear and saw the extent of his injuries. Just like him, he had bandages all over his body, but the wounds on his arms were the worst.

The former leader of the Mapiyan pointed to Spirit Bear's arms and he responded, "Burned by the explosion that Sen-hi barely survived. The Doctors here tell me I will most likely lose the use of my arms if they do not heal within a week. They tell me you, though, will carry those scars the rest of your life but that you will live."

The two men turned as one of the warriors that had lost the grip of the power of Shadow passed behind them, a look of defeat very apparent on his face as he looked at his former leader's state of being.

"You are to be taken to a trial for your actions, brother.", Spirit Bear sighed, leaning on a crutch he was given.

"A white man's trial.", the wounded Proud Eagle replied in defeat.

"They have total victory, old friend. And I helped them. All they needed was an excuse for taking our land and my actions were reason enough, I warrant.", he added.

"Your actions were a product of your madness, brought upon by their encroachment, their barbarism and treacherous ways, but they were your actions."

"You sound like you sympathize with..."

"No, brother, do not misunderstand.", Spirit Bear interrupted, looking at one particular cot that held a white soldier, beaten and bloodied, being tended by a woman and child.

"The dark powers bewitched you to their ways, used your anger and hatred of the white man to exact their purpose. But make no mistake that it was your hatred that brought this upon us. Hatred that was built and stoked by the fires of the white man's kingdom building. No outside forces.", he said finally.

Proud Eagle looked at him with confused eyes as he explained, "My companion once told me that in order to succeed in her beliefs, in her style, she had to let go of all extraneous forces, all 'outside forces'. Seeing her fight and being with her all this time has taught me that focusing on your inner spirit is the most important thing you could do."

"I focused on my spirit, brother, look what it did for me!", his eyes awash with new tears.

"You focused on the dark god's spirit, let it invade and consume you and your spirit. You became the outside force."

The realization of that truth hit Proud Eagle like an arrow to the heart.

"It will take time to heal the wound you inflicted upon your spirit, brother, but perhaps we can heal it together."

"As brothers.", his eyes met Spirit Bear's and the Shaman smiled, taking his friend's hands in his and embraced him.

"As a people."

SEN-HI SAKEDA WILL RETURN IN SWORD OF TIME

THE END

Printed in the United States
By Bookmasters